The Rambling of Rose

Melody Fisher

Other titles by this author

The Wishing Bones

Dedication

For all the wonderful people who I
love, you have all influenced me: I
hope in the right way!

Contents

Acknowledgements

To Gill, this little story is your fault. You encouraged, motivated, inspired and stimulated me and didn't let me give in. If you like it then it's been a pleasure, if you don't then I blame you!

For the other very nice people who read my previous offering and gave constructive, helpful and sound criticism and advice, I thank you.

For the circle of support I receive every day from my very valuable friends and relations, it's not taken for granted, I appreciate each one of you.

Chapter One

Thursday evening, I've got just short of an hour to get into Costrights, get my shopping, get home and out again to take Joan out.

Mental note to myself, cotton wool, frozen veg, chicken fillets, birthday card for Joan and pair of tights as my last pair, the ones I've got on, I put a hole in just above the back of my knee this afternoon. Repeating this mantra I grabbed a basket from the foyer of my local supermarket and without hesitation headed for "Birthday Cards" at a rate which would have made Usain Bolt jealous.

Birthday card done, even though I had to buy a card for 80 year old Joan which was festooned with cute bunnies as it was the best of the dismal selection on display. A card with a group of senior citizens playing poker for a bottle of gin would have been more fitting but there were none of that persuasion.

Grab cotton wool, haven't got time to work out what is the best deal today, now on to tights, easy, I'll be home with enough time to change clothes before picking up Joan to take her to the cinema to see the latest instalment of the Fifty Shades franchise, which is what she asked for as a present, when I asked if she was sure she replied with the euphemism, "Just because I can't afford the prices of the goods doesn't mean I can't look in the windows". Good on her.

So mental list, birthday card tick, tights tick,

cotton wool tick, chicken fillets next, so over to fridges at the far side of the shop. Blast! I've just seen Marie, I just don't have time for her today. I like her, I like her a tremendous amount but she can talk for England and I know she's just had her first grandchild and I will be at least an hour before I get the first word in. Thing is, I would love to hear all about what's happening, and see the photos, just not now!

I can see the chicken fillets I want, but I have to cross one of the supermarket aisles which is typically now completely empty of people and Marie is hesitating at the end of the aisle at the far end. What else did I want, if I can get that and come back for the chicken fillets, she may have moved on. So what was it, I look into my shopping basket and I just cannot bring to mind the missing article, I do this all the time, why didn't I write it down? That programme that used to be on TV, The Generation Game, had the conveyor belt with the prizes you used to have to remember within a certain time, if I had been a contestant on it, all I would ever have ended up with would have been the hostess trolley and a cuddly toy as more than two thoughts in my head at a time causes a complete shutdown. I am told it is to do with the menopause, shouldn't it be womenopause? Men, they have to get in everywhere, even something that has absolutely nothing to do with them has to be named after them. It does makes you irritated, fractious, bad tempered, ill, tired, fed up and touchy, on second thoughts being named after men makes absolute sense.

Yes, yes Marie's moved! With turbo speed from my starting position, the fillets are in my basket and I am over the next aisle, slightly out of breath and my heart pounding a little too generously in my chest, and she didn't see me. This feels very unkind as Marie is lovely but you cannot say, "I can't stop" to Marie, because that phrase takes her 45 minutes to digest.

Now I need to remember the missing thing and manoeuvre myself around the aisles with a stealth in keeping with the SAS, so as not to meet Marie. I will text her later, just to try to absolve myself of the guilt I am feeling. I trot down another aisle and into the, "Frozen Foods" section. "Peas" I say out very loudly, and the aisle which had been completely empty two seconds before is now so crowded, it's like Jason Statham has appeared and is giving out autographed thongs. Several people look over and I get a sympathetic smile from a lady who obviously has the same condition. I smile back relieved, I am not alone.

I have to lean in the chest freezer to pick up the last packet of, "Frozen Petit Pois with 30% extra free" at an unbelievable price of 50p which I drop into my basket and then I see another packet wedged under the,

"Seasonal sprouts with slithers of bacon and a cranberry jus" in the next tray along. I never liked sprouts and they have the unfortunate effect on me of unlimited wind within a couple of hours of eating them. Last time I had any, which was a Christmas dinner with my then in-laws, I was able to give a rendition of, "When the Saints Go Marching In" without an instrument or leaving my seat, all through the power of natural evacuation.

I shuffle along the freezer and manage to get hold of the corner of the packet, I'm leaning so far in that my skirt has ridden up to an uncomfortably short length and the hole in my tights has just decided to run all the way up to the gusset.

Just then a booming voice slices through the supermarket's version of, "Hound Dog" sung by Ellis Pelvisley with an announcement. This completely startles me and takes me off guard, my sensible shoe slips on the polished supermarket floor and at the same time an intense pain floods my chest and goes down my left side. I nose dive into the frozen sprouts, my arms forced out behind me like a jumbo jet and my feet leaving the floor as the weight of me follows my face into the freezer.

Pain searing through me, my chest is feeling like it is in a vice being tightened with all the tenacity of a Victorian woman trying to get her 30 inch waist to a modest 18 inch corset. My natural reaction was to grab my chest but I couldn't move my arms. I didn't have the energy to call out and when I opened my mouth, a frozen sprout fell in it, I must have split the packet when I hurtled into the freezer. Trust me, I couldn't fall into the cheesecakes or the chocolate eclairs.

Then, the pain just went, and I felt nothing. My nose, which was so cold it felt like a Yeti had hold of it, regained its normality. My chest stopped hurting and even the uncomfortable way that my body had bent backwards like a banana felt completely natural. "Rose!" A voice from the left side of me. Oh no it was Marie. "Rose, what are you doing?"

"Honestly Marie what do you think I'm doing, I don't make a habit of swan-diving into freezers, help me out". I said the words spitting out the frozen sprout but there was no reaction from Marie. Then a supervisor from the Customer Service desk came over, her name badge states "Alyce" what a strange way to spell Alice, at least it's a proper name, not a made up name from where the child was conceived and the latest Disney princess hyphenated together, like Snowdonia-Aurora, Rapunzel-Serengeti or Elsa-Trossachs. Still, I must be important for her to leave her counter, I thought they were chained to it, when you need help they conveniently look the other way and become engrossed in some paperwork in front of them, that is until a store manager walks past and then they are all smiles and bounce about like Jack-in-the-boxes. Another announcement on the loud speaker, "Can a First Aider come to Frozen Foods please". Oh how embarrassing and I am never going to make it on time to Joan's now.

Surprisingly Marie is quiet, which is a first for her. The First Aider and Alyce try to lift me out of the freezer. The bag of peas has adhered itself to my face via the ice and I am trying to breathe through a plastic bag. Funnily enough this doesn't bother me at all and I also have no strength and am unable to help in any way, my legs will not work and although the First Aider is speaking to me, "What's your name, and what happened to you?" I am answering, albeit muffled, but he is not taking any notice. The First Aider or, "Mike" as Alyce referred to him is offering reassuring words and I keep telling him I am fine. Each of them takes an arm and put it over their shoulders and they then heave me out. I carry a little extra weight and Alyce is on the slight side so once she has half my weight on her tiny frame she cannot support me and the result is her legs buckle under my weight and we all fall to the floor and I land on top of her and Mike on top of me, his aftershave is enough to destroy the ozone layer on its own.   Mike is wearing, "Stench" as endorsed by some celebrity who probably uses it to clean out his drains. The bag of peas ruptures during this process and hundreds of little petit pois roll all over the aisle. Can this get any worse? By this time a suitable audience has gathered, as respectable as for any busker in the town. I wondered should I give a chorus of "Oops up side your head" to lift the occasion but decide against it as Alyce is squirming around underneath me.

The cavalry has arrived!   A handsome couple of young paramedics wheeling a stretcher and carrying a bag comes into view. The crowd opens only a little to let them through and then closes around them again like a Venus fly trap. This production is obviously far better than anything on the TV tonight. Autographs later people.

Chapter Two

I was then aware of something. I was looking at myself on the floor! I wasn't laying on the floor, I was standing next to Marie but I was seeing my size 16 body, which I had kidded myself was a generous size 14, laying unceremoniously star fish like, looking like I was about to make snow angels on Costrights polished tiles. I look at Marie, she's gazing at the me that's on the floor, with her mouth open wide and for a change nothing coming out of it.

I lay towards the end of the aisle next to the offending freezer, in close proximity to Costrights Café (Homemade Food the Costright Way) and at right angles to the last check-out till. Customers of the Café are craning their necks to see what is going on, their view somewhat marred by the shopping brigade which had closed ranks around me like the Siege of Antwerp.

My basket lies unwanted at the side of my body and quick as a flash a lady with a permed hairdo with a slightly blue tone pilfers my basket and takes the last packet of Petit Pois 30% free. Alyce gives her a daggers look to which the lady responds, "Well she's dead now, she isn't going to need it and it's the last packet" which although true is a bit harsh considering the situation.

So I'm dead, it's a bit of an anti-climax to be honest. No last minute dying words, no confessions, no weeping relatives huddled round to hold my hand. I have just met my end in the freezer of Costrights and all anyone is concerned about is what I have in my shopping basket.

I look around and am drawn in the direction of the café for some reason. Diners can see me laying prostrate on one side of the café and on the other side is a large window which looks onto the car park. It's getting late, and darkness is starting to fall. I glance at the clock, I should be setting out for Joan's now, bless her, and she will be worried. Not many people will be. I haven't got a partner, the few friends I have include Marie and I was ready to dodge her as I didn't want to speak to her today. I can see a single tear welling in her eye and wonder if that's for me or if her contact lenses are playing her up again. I wish I could say something to her now.

My daughter Maisie will be upset when she hears the news. She was the best day's work I ever did, the production of which I will take full credit. The three second contribution of the sperm donor, my ex-husband, requires as much glossing over as possible. Maisie was 3 months old and he still couldn't remember her name, kept calling her Marnie, I called him by several monikers and not one of them was his name. My ex-husband could never remember anything, my handbag would have to cover every eventuality when we went out and then he would moan about how large my bag was but would whine if I forgot to bring his screwdriver/gloves/nose spray/glasses/spot welding tool etc. It was fortunate that his testicles were in a sac otherwise he would forget those as well.

I looked after Maisie pretty much all by myself, on little money, my marriage having broken down by the time she was six. Once, she came home from school and the sole of her shoe had come away from the upper leaving a flappy piece. The other kids at school had called her, "Flipper" and she was upset. There was no way I could afford new shoes so I had to repair them as best I could. That night, sitting in my shorty nightie I got out the super glue and pieced the shoe together as well as I could, being extremely careful not to get my fingers stuck to it. I had to hold the parts together tightly for a moment or two so I sat with the shoe gripped between my knees until I thought it was set. It was a marvellous job and the shoe was as good as new. Unfortunately I had stuck my knees together, so after a very uncomfortable night, the next day I had to waddle like a duck ready to lay an egg down to the doctor's surgery, a coat thrown over my nightie, to be greeted by a smirking receptionist. Final humiliation, having my knees prized apart, whilst the doctor looked at the slogan on my nightie which said, "Relax, don't do it" to which he replied, "We could probably market this as a contraceptive".

I am sure that episode coloured Maisie's life and on a subconscious level it has stayed with her. I would have liked her to have pursued a career which would have secured her a good future, as a lawyer or in the medical profession, she however decided to sell flip flops from a kiosk on a beach in Phuket but she is very happy, which is all I really want for her.

It's Pensioner's Day in the café. Cottage pie and rhubarb crumble with custard for the price of £3.99 which includes a glass for them to put their dentures in while they suck in the gloop which masquerades as food. One or two of them have returned to their gruel but the majority are still doing impressions of giraffes looking over at me. "She don't look that old," one of them says to her friend,
"Never know when it's going to take ya." says the other,

"Looks like her roots needed doing, her hair has the skunk look, black at the roots and blonde at the bottom. I wouldn't be seen dead like that".

"She obviously doesn't mind" said the other and raucous laughter ensued. Really, how rude, they talk about the younger generation, which is everyone as these gals are seriously old, and these old biddies are taking the mickey out my body laying just a few feet away.

Old people outnumber the rest of the population by about four to one in the small town where I live, correction, used to live. It's so common that the shop windows are bifocal. I had promised myself that when I got old I would do all the things that really annoy me about senior citizens. Oh not all over 65's are bad, but the few that are really make up for the others.

I had planned, when I had got to advanced years to buy one of those shopping trolleys on four wheels and then stand right in the doorway of shops talking endlessly to my friends so you cannot get in or out and I would glare at anyone who politely asked me to move. I wanted to drive one of those mobility scooters whilst carrying a broom crossways, so I could clear the path of pedestrians, satisfaction gained by leaving neat lines through just like cutting the grass. I wanted to have a really big shopping trolley and leave it at an angle to the aisle whilst I debated the difference between Oxo cubes and gravy granules. I wanted to turn up 5 minutes before the bank shuts when I've had all day to come in, to sort out a long winded problem, and keep the people waiting who only want to pay in a cheque. So many quests yet to fulfil. I really feel short changed, what a bugger.

The paramedics now bring out the big guns, the defibrillator is primed ready for use, and my blouse is unbuttoned and, oh horror,

I'm wearing my grey comfy bra. It was a toss-up between perky bright pink and lacy called, "Mystic" by Annabelle at Boobalicious or cuddly, flaccid old faithful, which would be the one I had chosen for today. It is clean, it just has seen better days and washing it with my extra thick thermal knee length culottes didn't help its colour. I had decided this would be its last wear. Ironically it looks like that has turned out to be true.

I once bought one of those lacy teddy arrangements. It looked really good on the super slim size 8 model who gazed wistfully at a Caribbean beach scene while twisting a strand of beautifully coiffured hair in her fingers. On me it was considerably lumpier as I have more boobage, very scratchy and I definitely had a larger size than a baby elephant. If I manufactured clothing I would reconfigure the sizes. You could be Exquisite, Magical, Sensational, Voluptuous or just Wow! The dreaded question, "What size Madam?" could be answered very confidently and proudly, "I'm Sensational!" wouldn't that feel great?

Once I purchased the teddy, I was keen to try it on. I needed a shoe horn to tuck in the parts of my body which bulged out the sides but when I was all encompassed in, I paraded around in front of the mirror. Unlike the model, I gaze out on a recycling centre over the road and in my enthusiasm I neglected to draw the curtains. Wilkie, the old boy who runs the place looked up and caught me prancing about like I was a nymph. Next time I looked out the window Wilkie stood there with his staff holding cardboard signs showing scores, 4, 3, 4 and 2 and grinning lecherously. Mortifying, though I am not sure whether I was more upset by the fact no one gave me a 5 or the fact that I had been seen.

The gusset of this garment felt like it was cutting my nou-nou like a cheese wire, but I persuaded myself that I looked good and it was worth the pain. After dressing in a pencil skirt and blouse, I bent down to feed the cat and the between-the-leg fastenings which were under significant strain gave way and the teddy flew up my back like a roller blind.

Chapter Three

This is weird, I don't feel anything, I can see my body but I'm not in it. I look down at my conscious self and can see my hands and legs, I'm not hazy or see through, and I look solid. I try and look into the glass of the freezer to see if I have a reflection, but I can't make anything out.

The throng about my body starts to wane and a couple of people now drift off, one of them straight through me. It felt like when you are a child in the back of a car which goes over a hump back bridge. The sort of feeling of leaving your stomach behind, not exactly pleasant, a strange sensation.

The paramedics are still fiddling about with my anatomy, the only time I get a good looking bloke interested in my person and I'm bloody dead!

So what happens now? Should I feel inner peace? Isn't there supposed to be a bright light somewhere that I walk into which envelopes me with love, warmth and the satisfaction that I am now going to see my long dead loved ones and meet the entity responsible for giving me a life in the first place. So what do I do, make an appointment? Surely they know I was going to arrive, it's a bit rude of them to be late. Angels, shouldn't my guardian angel greet me? Is there a queue I join? Do I take a ticket and a seat? Perhaps you don't go anywhere, you just stay existing in a different realm but watching everyone. I wonder if you can leave the place where you expired, or am I resigned for eternity wandering around the aisles and shelves of Costrights, my penance endlessly looking for bargains and money off.

I sit on the edge of the freezer swinging my legs, no one's going to tell me to move. The paramedics are doing a wonderful job, one of them gets interrupted by a short-sighted woman who mistakes him for a Costrights' employee and asks him where the dumpling mix is. He answered that he doesn't know, she doesn't hear him and steps closer, trips over my leg and hits her head on the corner of the freezer, the result being a squirt of blood evocative of the water displays outside the casinos in Las Vegas. Mayhem ensues with the husband of said lady saying he is going to report Costrights to Health and Safety for having a dead body lying about. There are peas, which have now defrosted and are being flattened on the floor, my body, two paramedics, one lady, plenty of blood, a stretcher, a defibrillator, a husband who is getting in the way, Alyce, Mike and now someone is now videoing the episode on their phone, probably ready to upload to You Tube, or send in to "You've been Framed" for £250. I glad I'm dead, it's wearing me out.

I see it, I see it, the bright light, and they have come for me, whoever they are. I will now get to answer for all my wrong doings during my 50 years on earth and serve whatever punishment is dealt out to me. I must walk into the light, does seem a little way away, I've got to trek over to the other side of the café to get to it but this must be it. Goodbye to this world.

I hop down from the freezer and walk, not glide, I thought perhaps I would be able to waft around but I may have to take a course on the, "Other side" to be able to do that. When I get into the light I may be handed a leaflet with various options, conversing with clairvoyants, themed, group and singular hauntings, poltergeist activity etc.

Section One – Beginners

Module 1 - Art of floating and levitation.

Module 2 - Delivering icy blasts of cold air.

Module 3 - Whispering and wailing.

Module 4 - Evaporation Techniques.

Module 5- Moving and hiding objects to cause maximum frustration to the living.

Once completing the above:

Qualification Level One - Haunting.

Onwards to the light. I observe the pensioner's meal package as I go. The cottage pie doesn't have much going for it but the crumble looks quite nice. I suppose my current status means I don't have to eat any more. Will that mean I lose weight, or will I stay the same? I notice I am still dressed in my same clothes, am I destined to carry on into perpetuity wearing my grey bra and a ladder in my tights or will I be bestowed of a pure white smock and wings? How do you get a halo, do you have to sit an exam for that or do you only get one if you have had a pure (boring) life, like nuns and religious people? I suppose I will shortly find out.

I take a last look at Marie who now looks whiter than I do. She is talking to Mike, "She was my friend, I saw her but didn't have time to speak to her today, poor Rose, trouble is she does go on a bit and I was only nipping in for langoustines".

You nip in for bread or milk, only Marie would nip in for langoustines, "and so I was trying to keep out of her way, I am a terrible person". Unbeknown to each of us, Marie and I had been playing hide and seek from each other in the aisles, how sad we are. Marie you are a lovely person, don't feel guilty for having human feelings.

I must get to the light, it may be on a timer

and if I don't get there within an allocated time frame my chance of everlasting peace will have vanished. I see the light flicker and I'm still the other side of the row of tables full of diners. My new status of undead has not enabled me to travel any swifter and I am loathe to walk through anything as I haven't got my ghost certificate yet.

I am within meters of the light, when I notice a lady wearing the same blouse as I have on. Apart from being dead I think it looks better on me. To think that this blouse was the last thing that I bought myself, had I known I would have splashed out and bought something else from Madam Fifi's.

Chapter Four

Madam Fifi's was one of those shops that had been impressive in its day. Owned by the same family since Noah built his ark. Madam Fifi's had previously sold ostentatious and flamboyant clothing and hats. In its heyday it supplied ladies with matching hat, gloves, shoes and handbag, as well as the outfit to wear them with. The grandeur had long since faded along with the youth of the sales assistants but the shop had continued to keep going, probably due to the grand-daughter's attempt to pull it into the current century by bringing in more modern pieces, which looked out of place against the traditional stock. I opened the door and it had one of those bells attached so any chance of a surreptitious look at the clothing was completely out of the question. I was greeted by Minette and Winette the two sisters who currently owned the shop who virtually pounced on me as I entered, eager for a sale.

Minette was wearing a calf length pink jersey dress with a blue belt, blue shoes and, even though she must be in her seventies, a blue bow in her white candy floss hair, she reminded me of the 1960's horror film "Whatever Happened to Baby Jane" with Bette Davis and Joan Crawford. If Minette was Bette Davis's character Baby Jane, Winette was definitely Joan Crawford's as Blanche, dressed in an exquisitely cut, but old fashioned skirt suit and crisp white blouse, with a mouth caked in pillar box red lipstick which had started to creep into the lines around her mouth. I felt like a mouse between two cats.

"Good Morning Madam", said Winette her elocution worthy of public school.

"What can we show Madam?" said Minette eager not to be left out. I may be wrong but I sense a rivalry between these two equal to the, "Baby Jane" film.

"I saw a shirt in the window and I wondered..." I didn't get time to finish as Winette had ushered me to the rail where the chosen garment was hanging. Minette was looking me up and down "Madam's size looks like an 18"

"16" I said a little too quickly and boldly. Minette gave me one of those old fashioned stares like a school teacher in a Dickens novel but removed the sizes 16 and 18 and gestured to the fitting room.

"This skirt would look very nice with the blouse, I think Madam should also try this".

Winette grabbed a skirt which looked like it would have been in fashion in 1910 and thrust it into my hand. I was too scared to object. I moved to the fitting room and was amazed when Minette came in with me. Tape measure around her neck, she was ready to take measurements for any alterations, a sign of old fashioned customer service. Winette thrust yet another hanger at me which this time was a very fluffy jumper. "To go over the blouse on chilly days" she said as if to explain.

It was a small changing room and with two people, a chair, three things to try on and a coat hook which was so fierce it could take your eye out, it was very cramped.

I was grateful when the bell jangled indicating another person had come into the shop. Minette, worried that Winette would get there first and her sale may be more successful, hurriedly said to me, "I will be back shortly Madam" and I was relieved.

It did mean that I would have to try on in record time and hopefully be out of the fitting room by the time she was back but I don't particularly like undressing in front of a complete stranger. Skirt was just a no, the only time it would be suitable was if I was a suffragette ready to chain myself to the door of a posh coffee shop to get them to lower their prices.

The blouse was pretty nice, and a good fit in the size 16 which I would be very happy to point out to Madam Minette. I could, through the chink in the changing room curtain, see that the sisters were engaged with a customer who looked like she was interested in multiple things. I took off the blouse and hung it back on the hanger. I decided to try on the fluffy jumper as Winnie and Minnie were busy. I pulled it on and it was really soft, I stroked the arm of it. I stood admiring myself in the mirror and saw a red blotch appear on my neck, I then felt a definite itchy feeling on my back. I was having a reaction to the material of the jumper. I needed to get it off. I tried to pull it over my head speedily but it seemed caught up on something, I managed to get the jumper up over my face, but it was tight which resulted in my arms being forced above my head and I flailed around looking like a sea anemone and I blindly bumped into the sides of the cubical. As I struggled and panicked it made me hot and I started panting, after what seemed forever I released an arm and was able to gulp a breath of fresh air. I turned around and the jumper, still tethered by something swung around with me. I peeked over my shoulder through the knit of the jumper and looked into the mirror and saw that the fluffy jumper was caught up on the hooks of my bra strap. I did the Argentinian tango trying to release the jumper but it did not budge and I could see that it was starting to pull the threads of the jumper. If I damaged it I would have to buy it and the price label stated an incredible £65.00! There was nothing else for it I would have to take off my bra to untangle the jumper. A quick look at Winnie and Minnie who were thankfully still persuading the customer to part with her cash. Off with the bra, I untangled the threads which mercifully hadn't pulled. Then I heard the bell jangle, I looked through the curtains, the customer had gone and both sisters were striding back to me. I stood there topless and couldn't find my bra at all, and it's not a little item, it could give Madonna's cone bra a run for her money. Panicked, I pulled on my own jumper, so at least I was decent whilst I searched around for my bra.

Winette threw open the curtain. I was truly glad no one else was in the shop it could have been embarrassing! "How did you get on?" she asked with a stare which could freeze vodka.

"I'll take the blouse." I muttered, still

looking cautiously round for my bra. Minette reached in and took the hanger with the blouse to the till, Winette followed her. I walked behind them both but glanced over my shoulder into my reflection in the mirror. What I saw made me pray for the heavens to open up and engulf me, I resembled Quasimodo as my bra had got hooked up on the inside of my own jumper and the cups were protruding down my back like some sort of dinosaur. I got my purse ready to pay as I needed to vacate that shop as soon as possible.

"Madam looks as if she has scratched herself" said Minette and both sisters peered a little too closely at the red slash which was galloping across my chest.

"Allergic reaction." I said meekly. I paid quickly and snatched the bag with the blouse, which I then threw over my shoulder hopefully hiding the augmentation projecting from my back and walked sideways like a crab out of the shop, keeping my back away from the sisters. The whole episode quite traumatized me.

Chapter Five

The light is causing me to turn my head away, it is so intense. All the films I have seen show it as a warm, soothing light which bathes you in an ambient glow to welcome you to another kingdom. This is a harsh, stinging light, which could give me a migraine. I look away and see blobs in front of my eyes, like looking at a lava lamp.

When my eyes return to ordinary vision again, I am looking directly at Oliver Sykes who I had a crush on when I used to catch the bus to college. Still ruggedly good looking but with considerably less hair. He is sitting with an equally good looking lady of similar age, a younger woman, a toddler and a baby. I made the assumption his wife, daughter and grandchildren. To me he looked quite content and was talking and laughing. I am so close to him I could touch him, something which in my teenage years I would have walked over hot coals to do. I never told him, he wouldn't have been interested in me, and I wonder should I have said something at the time? Even now I cringe at the awkwardness, not that that is reserved for teenagers, I had my fair share as an adult.

After I divorced I lived a solitary and celibate life until Maisie was about twelve. Then the girls with whom I worked at the office encouraged me to start dating again. This was a very nerve racking and horrific experience, much worse than when I was young. Older daters have so much baggage, both emotional and physical, something the girls had no knowledge of. It was so much simpler for them, no children or ex-husbands to juggle. Their love lives were a constant revolving door of men, and they were always on the look-out for the next one before finishing with the present one. On-line dating websites and phone Apps are completely alien to me. I'm a technophobe and the modern age is such a mystery to me. I learn the minimum I can get away with in order to do my job. As for dating, I prefer the old fashioned method, wanting to find out about a potential mate through going out for a few weeks rather than having a complete resume posted on line.

Against my better judgement I allowed Rachel, a lovely young girl with whom I really got on well despite the massive age gap between us, to set me up on a date via some technical wizardry she had on her phone. This subject afforded Rachel and our other colleagues Sara and Laura much hilarity and amusement and so many times before the actual assignation I wanted to cancel but I was persuaded to continue.

The day arrived. Laura told me to wear something I could get off and on easily just, "In case" I got an opportunity and presented me with a pair of knickers with, "Use by" and the days date emblazoned across the front which I regarded with distaste, which fuelled the sniggering of the girls further.

The girls recommended a lunch time date to begin with in a crowded place and to have a definite cut off for the date to end. I didn't remember it being this complicated when I was younger. Knowing how anxious I was, it was agreed that the girls would have a table strategically placed a few away from me. One of them would text me with a, "Danger" text after about 10 minutes to ensure I was safe and willing for the date to continue and if I was happy I would signal, and they would leave us to it, otherwise one of them would interrupt and under some pretext take me away. I appreciated they were looking out for me but was it all organised so they could watch which did make me even more nervous.

My mouth dropped open when I saw Simon in the flesh. He was absolutely gorgeous. Tall, blond, blue eyed, polite, muscular, dressed impeccably, just film star quality all the way through. I glanced over at Rachel and the girls and they had massive grins on their faces and were giving me rude gestures when he came over to the table. I looked down at my phone which was on silent to see a text from Rachel just stating, "I would!"

He was enchanting. Why was this man on a dating website? Why on earth did he agree to meet me? I relaxed significantly in his company, so much so that I didn't even see the, "Danger" text Rachel sent me and after the first few minutes I was so engaged in conversation I forgot my spectators were there.

All was going so well. Simon tried to attract the attention of one of the waiting staff but when this failed he said he would go up to the counter as he was aware that I had a limited time as I was on my lunch break. He needed to go past me in order to access the counter and I had put my posh new handbag on the floor near my foot but nearest the aisle. This bag was my pride and joy, ultra-expensive and this was its first outing. A beautiful maroon leather with a silk lining and large round handles which were easy to get hold of and it had a popper clasp not a proper full length zip. Simon smiled as he walked passed, but then his expression changed as he caught his foot in the handle of my bag and similar to a child's skipping toy my handbag rotated round his ankle , the momentum carrying it onward tripping up his other foot as he staggered to try and save himself. His handsome face contorted into something which resembled a gargoyle and his chin collided with the table, resulting in the table upturning. Not content with this, the fates decreed that the contents of my handbag scattered in the vicinity, sending tampons cascading in a very neat arc around the debacle.

Silence, only the sound of the floor opening up to swallow me, then guffaws of laughter from a certain table. Simon ever charming but with a swollen lip excused himself but graciously paid the bill for the drinks. I might as well have been sitting in a shop window of the red light district in Amsterdam as all eyes were on me. I picked up the offending tampons and put them back in my posh handbag and with as much dignity as I could muster, which wasn't much, I walked out and I never, ever, went back to that restaurant and I never again used that handbag.

You would think that that incident would have put me off dating for good but some months later I arranged my own date via an online facility without any help or knowledge of my work colleagues. The unfortunate consequences of my last date didn't detract from the fact that Simon had been lovely in every way and I hoped that misfortune would not befall me again.

My next date was at the cinema. I decided to have my hair cut and styled for the occasion and I was quite satisfied with it when I left the salon in the afternoon and I treated myself to some new make-up from the department store in the high street. The girl who served me was wearing so much make up on her face I am surprised she had anything left to sell, but she persuaded me to buy a new lipstick called "Cherished by you" and a super ultra-expensive mascara and as I left the shop I was feeling positive. By the time it was time to go out in the early evening my hairstyle had dropped a little but it still looked nice and I felt I was, "Rocking the look" as Rachel would say. I had had several inches cut off the bottom and some wispy strand effects going on about my face which did annoy me as they kept tickling me and I was performing the sideways blow from the corner of my mouth to keep them away from my eyes.

The date progressed very nicely, a drink before we went in, then to the cinema and settle down to watch a thriller type drama. The company was good, the film was good, I felt good but it wasn't to last. A particular strand of hair was driving me mad and it was too short to go behind my ear and too long to stay sticking out, it curled round and kept poking me in the eye. A weepy eye is not a good look when you are wearing a new mascara and I was anxious not to look like a panda when we emerged from the darkness.

In temper I put up my hand to push the irritating hair away, just at the very moment my date leaned in to give me a furtive kiss on the cheek. Result, my index finger went right up his nostril. I don't know who was more surprised. Horrified I jerked forward muttering all kind of apologies and with my other hand upset my date's drink which he tipped into his lap. The ice cubes gathered at his crotch which was a shock and caused him to shout out a couple of expletives and he stood up. This was causing quite a commotion and someone called an attendant and amid jeering from the rest of auditorium seats we vacated the cinema to the strains of, "I think I'd better leave right now" by Will Young playing on the internal loudspeaker.

Chapter Six

I wish I'd been a bit more adventurous. Now I'm not going to get the chance to travel the world, write a book, stand for election or even visit Maisie in Phuket. I should have taken some chances, been a bit more extreme, had outrageous haircuts, been more assertive, and not been afraid of everyone else. I admire those people who just go for it now I'm done for it.

I did stand up for myself once. I earned myself an accolade from Maisie, for it she was in awe of me which is a great achievement in the eyes of a then teenager. I have always worked in office jobs, generally I have met some lovely, funny, kind and wonderful people, some of who became good friends, at other times I came across people who I would quite happily burn at the stake.

I used to work for a business which required me to visit the post office several times a week. My workplace was a little office in the countryside and so the post office was also rural. In order to complete the necessary transactions for the task it was mandatory that a form was completed for every application which was taken in to the post office. Sometimes I took just one form other times it was six or more. As it was a laborious and protracted task to fill in these forms I had a supply on my desk and I would go to the post office readily prepared. Each form could take 10 minutes to complete and then a further 5 minutes for the post master to action, therefore it could take a little time.

The post office had a shop attached and was owned by a slug of a man who didn't actually want to do anything. He sat on a stool and gruffly issued orders to his assistant who ran around trying to please him and never succeeded He peered over his glasses like I was beneath him and he was doing me the utmost honour by speaking to me, never a greeting or kind word, it was a real effort for him to speak at all but I always made the effort, "Kill with kindness" my Nana used to say. This situation had been going on for a least a couple of years. One day I walked in with a massive smile and said a rapturous "Good Morning" as I approached the counter. I handed over my forms and there were a lot on this day. He thrust them back through the hatch and said,

"These are now illegal do them again" with

as much grace as you would expect from this Neanderthal. Politely I ask,

"Why?"

"Forms changed this morning" was the grumpy reply, "I knew this was going to happen last week." the expression on his face was smug.

"You knew last week, you saw me take some forms yesterday and you didn't feel able to say anything? Couldn't you have let me know?" I felt a tinge of rage creeping in.

"Not down to me to do your job." was the ever gracious reply. I don't know why but on this day I was not going to be spoken to like that. I don't know where it came from but the odious little man had it coming.

"Why do you have to be such a nasty, horrible, lazy and incredibly vile man? I have been coming here for two years and have always been pleasant and polite to you even though your responses would make an ape look as if it had etiquette. You have never even said hello to me let alone pass the time of day. Your shop is always empty, have you ever wondered why? You would need a crow bar in order to lift your sizable posterior off that stool, I have never seen you actually move, are you welded to the seat? You make your poor assistant run around for you giving her orders while you wallow in your seat.

I am going to stand at this counter and complete these forms ready for you to process them. If it takes me a couple of hours I will continue to stand here and do them, if you are lucky enough to get another customer, I will explain why I am holding them up and I will ask them their opinion. I will not move away from this counter until it is done because as you quite correctly pointed out, it's not down to you to do my job, not that you would get my job as it needs courtesy and consideration, two elements which you do not possess".

Neanderthal man just stared at me. I completed the forms and handed them one by one to be processed, which he did, with as much charm as ever, I even managed to point out when he made an error. I left that establishment with a newly attained confidence.

When I got back to my office I had been gone a considerable length of time and I was called into the Managing Director's office at once. Neanderthal man had rung to complain about me and banned me from his post office and shop forever and demanded that my M.D. send someone else in future. My M.D. to his credit supported me, as he too had had experience of this appalling little man, furthermore the M.D. instructed that no one from the business where I worked would in future use his services. The only reprimand I got, if you can call it that was, "Rose, we don't have many Post Offices around here, please don't get banned from any more of them!"

A week later I was shopping in town and a lady I kind of recognised waved to me and negotiated the traffic to talk to me. It took a little while then I realised this was Neanderthal's assistant. "I hoped I would see you" she said, "I heard what you said and was willing you to say more, I was standing behind the curtain listening to every word. I've told most of the people in the village, you've become a sort of legend, everyone has been laughing about it. He started to have a go at me when you left and I found courage and thought of you and told him where he could stick his job. It felt great".

I've been described as a lot of things, "Legend" is not one I think I am worthy of but if this lady found inner strength because of me and told this bully where to go I feel gratified in my actions. Strangely enough the shop only lasted another four months after that and closed, must have been co-incidence though. There is an old saying,

"Always be nice to everyone on the way up as you may just meet them on the way down". I think I am ok as he was already on his way down.

Chapter Seven

I heard a mobile phone ringing, the distinctive bars of the theme from "Mission Impossible" rang out from the handbag on the floor next to my dead body. Never had that ringtone seemed more apt. It was probably Joan. I could imagine her all dressed up and anxiously waiting for me at "Heaven's Gate" the old people's home in which she had her own, "Little cell" as she referred to her accommodation. No one answered my phone and it rang off, I could imagine a terse voicemail from Joan.

Heaven's Gate is actually a rather lovely place. The staff are absolutely wonderful, so many old people's homes and care homes are lambasted and criticized for the care they give, with the accommodation being neglected, failing equipment and overworked staff who only stay a short while. Heaven's Gate does not fall into that category. Joan's "Little cell" is well equipped with an en-suite shower room, super soft carpet, nice décor although Joan can add touches as she feels fit. Her room is so large she could entertain if she wished as there is space for her bed and a table with two chairs and another armchair. Joan has her own TV in the room for when she wants time alone but the latest 56" screen TV is in the communal lounge, and another smaller room also has a TV and a DVD library for the use of the "Inmates" as Joan refers to herself. Although she constantly depicts it as a prison she's very happy there and can come and go as she pleases.

I used to try and visit Joan a couple of times a week, one night in the week and an afternoon at the weekend if possible. I would sometimes take her out or even just sit with her and talk to the other residents.

Joan had an admirer 83 year old Richard Bird called Dickie for obviously reasons who constantly went down on one knee to propose and then had to have help to get up again. The staff pleaded with Joan to say yes to him so they wouldn't have to keep helping him up. There was Jeremy a retired gardener, the twin sisters Ophelia and Octavia, who had rooms adjacent to each other and who bickered continuously and even resorted to physical tussling on occasion. One sister, Octavia had married and had five children but Ophelia had remained single. Both sisters had worked at the same place which had been in the kitchens of the local convent school. They had a regular visitor Sister Mary Theresa, but they would get jealous if Sister Mary

Theresa wanted to talk to anyone else. There was Klepto Kitty who, although a really nice lady would find homes for articles which were, "left out". Each night there was a search of her room to return items back to their original owners. One time, a particularly fruitful day for Kitty yielded a book, three pairs of spectacles, a bus pass, a Lego helicopter, various magazines, a jar of jam, a hamster and a truss in an attractive shade of lilac. They never did find the owner of the truss!

Ophelia and Octavia would hold court sitting in the bay window, as they could see everyone approaching from the driveway to the building and everyone coming in the main doors. Woe betide any unsuspecting new occupant who dared to sit in their seat. Nothing would be said but the ladies would sit either side and stare at the unfortunate individual until they were so uncomfortable that they would move. As soon as the occupant was aware of the hierarchy the ladies would be gracious as ever and nothing would ever be said, but as far as they were concerned the benchmark had been set.

Every Thursday Sister Mary Theresa would visit and they would sit in the window seat surrounding the round table. The residents called them, "The Three Coventeers" although not to their faces. I think there actual names were more amusing Mrs. Octavia Lorde and Miss. Ophelia Blessed. The names on their respective doors reading, "O Lorde and O Blessed."

Ophelia had started to forget things and although she was a very knowledgeable and intelligent woman certain words started to escape her, much to her frustration, although much worse was the habit she now had of using the wrong, inappropriate word to describe something. Octavia was looked upon to translate on these occasions.

As the sisters used to work in a kitchen many conversations would centre on the food which was served in Heaven's Gate. Ophelia was describing a recipe to Octavia and Sister Mary Theresa which needed the meat to be "Urinated in sauce overnight".

"You mean marinated" said Octavia,

"I know what I mean" said an indignant Ophelia, "I mesmerized all the recipes, all in my head" she said tapping her forehead,

"You mean memorised" said Octavia, a stern look from Ophelia, who continued,

"You have to be careful when leaving meat to stagnate as all the orgasms can alter the flavour".

"Ophelia, I don't think that's what you mean" interjected Octavia looking at an embarrassed Sister Mary Theresa.

"I know what I mean!" said a frustrated Ophelia in a loud voice.

"Shall we have a drink?" inquired Sister Mary Theresa thinking to dilute the situation.

"Yes I want some of that posh stuff, prosthetics"

"Prosecco" said Octavia rolling her eyes which unfortunately Ophelia noticed and then prodded her sister in the shoulder, the reaction of Octavia was to prod her back and then what can only be described as a scuffle ensued with Sister Mary Theresa trying to separate them which was brave of her as a referee at a wrestling match would have thought twice. A voice from ex-bookmaker Barry at the side of the room called out,

"I'll give you three to one on Octavia for a knock-out".

Dickie replied, "No evens, cos there's Nun between them." the men chortled and continued with their banter.

On another occasion I saw who I thought was another new resident. An elegant slim lady with the most beautifully cut clothes and expensive accessories sashayed her way through the lounge and out to sit in the conservatory. There was something vaguely familiar about her but I just assumed I had seen her before in Heaven's Gate.

Joan, with whom I was sitting, asked, "Do you know who that is?"

"I can't place her Joan, but I didn't see her properly. Gorgeous clothes, obviously designer and those shoes, did you see them? Have I already met her?" I said racking my brain to recall the lady,

"No you haven't met her, I'll call her over so I can introduce you" offered Joan. I picked up a mischievous kind of look.

"Jenny, Jenny" called out Joan, "Come and meet Rose". Jenny turned and smiled, uncrossed her legs, got up and walked towards us. I sensed Joan watching my every move as Jenny approached. My drab outfit screamed out, "I can't be bothered" in comparison to Jenny's and I felt very self-conscious in my casual trousers and T-shirt.

Jenny sauntered towards me like a catwalk model, beautifully and fastidiously if rather heavily made up. The smile she gave me with her dental implants was similar to the advertisements for whitening teeth treatments and nearly blinded me". Realisation dawned and there is no way I could disguise my expression, shock, astonishment, amazement, none of these adjectives accurately describe the completely moronic look on my face.

"Hello Jer, Jennery" I stuttered trying to conceal any awkwardness on my part, but failing miserably,

"Where are you going today looking lovely Jenny" said Joan, with not a trace of sarcasm or irony,

"I'm going out for the day. Daytrip to the coast. I used to go when I was a child and I want to see how it's changed." I bet you've changed more was my initial bitchy thought.

"Oh I can see my transport now. Must go, tell you about it later" and with that Jenny disappeared out the door.

"Joan that was cruel" I said looking at her whilst Joan grinned back at me, "I was totally unprepared for that",

"It was fun to see your face" she replied wickedly. "Jeremy is Jenny on Wednesdays I thought you knew," said Joan loving every minute of this. "apparently when Jeremy's wife was alive she knew of his, umm, his." Joan hesitated trying to find the right word "his hobby" was all she could come up with, "and although she was fine with it she didn't want to see it so he could only dress up on a Wednesday when she went to see her friend. The proviso which she stated was each time Jeremy bought something for Jenny he had to buy something for his wife of equal value so I think she did ok out of it. When his wife died he had more money to treat himself, but he only ever becomes Jenny on a Wednesday. You can tell he definitely doesn't stint himself when he's Jenny, stingy as anything as Jeremy though".

"Is everyone at Heaven's Gate all right with this?" I asked curiously,

"It's not really a problem" said Joan, "The fellas all like Jeremy, he was head gardener up at Hallgreen and they like hearing his stories about the toffs and about gardening of course. Norman, the new bloke in here for respite care doesn't like him but he doesn't like anybody and no one much cares for him either, and the women like Jenny because she lets them borrow her gorgeous handbags and accessories for going out, provided of course that it's not on a Wednesday when he may wish to use them. Ophelia's a bit funny about it but Octavia thinks it's jealousy for the fine things Jenny has. Klepto Kitty loves Jenny but a lot of blingy type things end up in her room if Jenny leaves anything unattended. Whether it's Jenny or Jeremy the person inside is a lovely soul and I couldn't give two hoots whether Jeremy wears a dress or not. He has a wicked sense of humour and he doesn't take offense".

I only once saw Octavia, Ophelia, Sister Mary Theresa and Jenny in a room at the same time. Sister Mary Theresa had changed her day to visit and was sitting with the twins in the bay window and they were watching one of the residents' grandchildren playing in the lounge. They were dancing to some music that was blaring out from the television and although it was a bit loud they were entertaining the crowd and the people looked on with smiles on their faces.

Jenny walked in and one of the children took her hand so Jenny started dancing with them, just the Ring-O-Roses type thing you do with small children but Ophelia was not in a good mood,

"Just who does she think she is? In her Manilla Blankets" Ophelia was off on one,

"Manolo Blahniks Ophelia" deciphered Octavia,

"Carrying her Herpes Handbag".

"Hermes, Ophelia".

"and dancing around to big erection"

"One Direction! Ophelia, ONE DIRECTION!" shouted Octavia but it was too late Sister Mary Theresa had fainted.

Chapter Eight

"Would you help Norman with his forms online Rose?   He's ok at providing the answers but he can't see too well and he gets bad tempered and frustrated with the computer and you would be doing us an enormous favour if you helped him out" I was asked,

"No problem, I'll get myself sorted and if you would like to send him over. I'll sit over there" I waved my hand to indicate the table in a more private spot.

"Thank you Rose, it is appreciated. Norman is a bit cantankerous and has unfortunately alienated some of the residents and half of them are not speaking to him, unfortunately it's the half that could have helped him" said Mrs. Collins one of the carers.

I settled myself. I used a laptop provided by Heaven's Gate to help several of the guests who do not have a computer or access to one or are just worried about using one. I am no expert but I will try to help, anything from ordering things online to looking up family history, it's just a little something I can do to help out sometimes.

I looked up just in time to see a figure appear in the doorway. My eyes closed so I was looking through a slit and like a scene from an old western, the large man standing in the doorway advanced towards me, although I recognised him straight away he didn't identify me until he had approached the table, what a lovely surprise for him. Neanderthal man! He looked at me and his face changed as he recollected where he had seen me before and when the penny dropped he took an audible gulp. I am ashamed to say I felt very satisfied by that.

As I am not a vindictive person, my friends may disagree with that statement, I felt I ought to clear the air between us.

"Hello Norman, remember me?" Not waiting for a reply I continued, "My name is Rose and I am very happy to help you, however, I will not be treated in the same way as you did before when I was a customer of yours. You will treat me with politeness, respect and on an equal footing, and I will afford you the same courtesy. No mention will be made of our previous encounters. If you cannot indulge me with ordinary good manners this meeting is over.

I trust you are in agreement with this?" I looked at him directly and smiled what I deemed to be a sweet smile.

Neanderthal Norman looked very uncomfortable and mumbled a response, "Sorry Norman I didn't hear that" I said loudly so that it was heard by the surrounding tables, I caught a muffled snigger from a table around the corner. I felt like a teacher with a petulant child but I was going to deal with this. A voice with restrained dignity said, "Rose, I am pleased to meet you and I would appreciate your help" said Norman.

"Norman what can I do for you?" was my reply. Ceasefire had been called.

Chapter Nine

So here I stand in Costrights experiencing my last moments in this domain. The light to which I am supposed to be drawn is now retreating, like it's backing away. No, No! Have I missed my turn? I've not been that long getting to it. I look over at my body, I do wish someone would pull down my skirt, I never showed that much leg alive and I don't see why it should be on show now. The hunky paramedic is still working on me, pity I won't be able to tell him how much I appreciate it.

Then a shooting pain, penetrating and forceful which would take my breath away if I still were breathing. Oh extreme pain, what is going on? I'm dead you are not supposed to feel any more pain are you? My physical body has just jerked and a force similar to a magnet is dragging me back.

Will I get to witness my own funeral I wonder? It will be really interesting to see who actually bothers to turn up and what they say about me really, not the stuff that is said in church but the little private conversations between the nubs of friends. Did generously endowed Jilly really forgive me for using her discarded wedding dress as a tepee for Maisie and although Carina said it was fine, was it really when Maisie who was seven at the time played hairdresser's with her and gave her waist length hair a lop-sided bob?

At fifty years of age I'd been to several funerals, all of them differing in ways but ultimately they end the same way. I remember one, the father of a close friend, who was a lovely man. The sun shone in through the stained glass windows of the church and cast patterns on the floor like a multi-coloured kaleidoscope and sparkled like a blanket over the coffin. The ceremony was uplifting and amusing, respectful and dignified just like the man and tears mingled with smiles but there was such a euphoric feeling which pulsed through the church. I had never felt that feeling before and I have never felt it since in those circumstances but it is one which I'd like to think, maybe someone will feel about me.

Not long after I met Jenny, although I'd met Jeremy many times, Joan rang me to impart the sad news that he had died, he had stumbled in his Manolo Blahniks and fallen hitting his head, he was taken to hospital and his daughter contacted. He never regained consciousness. His daughter, who lived miles away managed to get to see him as he laid in his hospital bed. She leant over to give him a last kiss and was surprised, and drew back sharply, looking at the nurse she had inquired, "Can you tell me why my father is wearing more lipstick than me?"

The next time I visited Heaven's Gate the sombre atmosphere filtered throughout the building both for the departed but also the residents taking stock of their own mortality.

Jeremy's funeral was to be on a Wednesday which did then fuel several conversations as to the outfit he should be buried in. Jeremy's shocked daughter had been filled in as to her father's preference for clothing on a Wednesday and had made her choice, no one dared ask her what she decided.

Following a spell of atrocious weather, the day of Jeremy's funeral was a bright December morning. Snow had been falling for several days but had stopped early in the morning of the funeral and the picture book setting of the church looked beautiful even though the reason for the visit was a sad one.

A crocodile of people made their way up the incline to the church door. On a summers day the gradient and camber of the path are not noticeable, but walking up the slope on this particular day proved very difficult and for Mrs. Collins, the carer from Heaven's Gate, pushing a resident in a wheelchair was a struggle.

Ophelia had decided she would speak at the funeral and regale the ensemble with some "Antidotes". When the vicar laughed and explained with a smile that an antidote was a little late in the present circumstances and that what she actually meant was an "Anecdote", Ophelia fixed him in a hostile stare and said, "An antidote is something that counteracts an unpleasant feeling. Saying goodbye to Jeremy is an unpleasant feeling. An anecdote is an interesting or amusing story about someone. If I tell a tale about Jeremy which is an anecdote it will become an antidote and lift the spirits of the people at the funeral. So antidote or anecdote it means the same in this instance". After that lecture the vicar knew when he was beaten and retreated. Ophelia was magnificent, she knew she had been caught out by using the wrong word but eloquently manipulated the situation. I really wish I had the verbal ability to turn around and end a conversation so succinctly in my favour.

As usual the service was followed by the interment. Filing out of the church following the immediate funeral party the mourners were stamping their feet trying to get the circulation going after sitting in a freezing church and then standing in snow. The vicar who would normally be at the front allowed Mrs. Collins out before him as the wheelchair was causing her some problems and in a small church was in the way of the exit. Once outside the pallbearer's were struggling with the weight of the coffin, the slant downwards of the path and after many people compacting the snow going into the church the slippery surface underfoot. The mourners were able to walk through the graves but this was not an option for the pallbearers who were trying to maintain decorum and dignify Jeremy's last journey of this world.

With confident strides the pallbearers walked towards a flat area to await the vicar who was required to be in front to lead the way. Tentatively everyone slipped and wobbled over the path to get behind the procession for the final walk to the graveside including the vicar. In his haste to attain his position he rallied quickly, a little too quickly and he moonwalked on the ice then performed a toe loop and a triple Sal chow equal to any ice dancing champion. Had his landing been on his feet he would have been awarded sixes across the board but regrettably his balance failed and resulted in him hitting the ground hard and acting as a human bowling ball. The pallbearers were eyes forward and had no chance to escape the missile in the shape of the vicar which came up from behind them and took their feet out from underneath them allowing the coffin to fall. Someone shouted, "Strike" I'm not sure who but it was not appropriate at that moment. If that wasn't enough the vicar carried on down the path on his backside, the unaccompanied coffin gathering speed, followed behind and resembled a toboggan with assorted pallbearers scattered like discarded skittles. The vicar skidded off track and collided with a tree, the coffin travelled further right down to the hole dug for its resting place and careered straight into it, the person who then shouted, "Hole in one" has not been identified.

There is not a suitable response to a

catastrophe such as this, on a day which should be for contemplation and remembrance. All eyes were focused on Jeremy's daughter who showed remarkable composure and then said very loudly, "I hope all this didn't crease the Chanel dress he's got on".

Chapter Ten

What-ever is that paramedic doing?   The piercing pain slicing through me is never ending and I thought this was my time for eternal peace.   I'm not good with medical stuff at the best of times and obviously this is not a good time.

Even ordinary check-ups would fill me with anxiety and trepidation and as a female every part of me had to have some type of check on a regular basis. Any female who has given birth will identify with the fact that you have no pride left afterwards. When Maisie was born I didn't care if the Coldstream Guards were in there with me as long as she came out. Not that you have to have a baby to be medically prodded and poked.

Once I reached the archaic age of 50 a new delight breezed through my letter-box in the form of an invitation for breast screening. Invitation? You get an invitation to a party, a wedding or some event which you should enjoy, look forward to and hopefully gain an uplifting experience. The only lifting going on is the nurse heaving my mammaries about, placing them in a vice and pressing them beyond recognition. I go in with melons and come out with pizzas.

The customary smear test is something which causes the hardest of women to shudder. It doesn't take long, it does save lives, and it is worth it, so why am I such a wimp to torture myself with the thought of it for days beforehand? The thought of the procedure is much worse than the process itself. A parent gives a child a treat when they have had to experience something uncomfortable and been good for the duration, why can't Doctors give women a voucher for 20% off a handbag when they have been good?

One year my smear test was booked in the middle of the afternoon.   Getting an appointment at a Doctor's surgery is like having a winning lottery ticket, so whatever is on offer you grasp. For someone who works office hours 3.15pm is a really awkward time, not lunchtime, not enough time to go home beforehand and not late enough to go straight home afterwards, so preparations have to be taken before hand. Bath in morning and stuffed into the pocket in my handbag where I keep my receipts, lipstick, sweets I've forgotten about that are sticky and covered in fluff and various oddments, I put an additional pair of knickers ready to change into.

I'd given myself enough time to sort myself out before the appointment and just when I was about to absent myself from my desk at work to freshen up in the Ladies I got detained by a someone who could win an Olympic medal for talking and wanted to discuss many subjects which needed a considerable amount of detail and follow up from my side. I was on the telephone for ages. Once I'd managed to extricate myself from the call, I was panicking I would be late and it was a mad dash to the Ladies to change my underwear, freshen up and rejuvenate my person by spraying a spot of the perfume I'd bought from a market stall, which should have resembled a famous fragrance by a premium brand which is named after a common white flower. I must have interpreted it incorrectly as the one I have is called, "Dayzie" by Frank & Scents and smells more like decaying cabbage or dandelion than a sweet daisy aroma, but at least I had made the effort to feel clean whilst being inspected.

I got to the surgery all ruffled and agitated and registered with a computerised screen, a faceless entity that takes my name and date of birth and instructs me to take a seat which I am grateful for as my hormones have decreed that Mount Vesuvius has picked this moment to erupt within my body. The surge of heat which travels up my torso is radiating so much heat that if harnessed could power the whole of East Anglia for a week. Anyone within a distance of a metre is sure to be singed as the boiling point of this 50 year old body has been reached and if I didn't cool down quickly my skin will be melting from my bones. I downed a cup of cold water from the dispenser and wished I could dive in it as I was puffing like a steam train. Being a female is utter rubbish, years of periods followed by years of hot flushes, mood swings, aching limbs and memory loss. Not content with that I've also sprouted whiskers on my upper lip and succumbed to the middle aged spread, which in my teens I genuinely thought was a margarine for adults.

It is while sitting there that my body informed me, I again, need the toilet, another age related thing. My head told me I cannot possibility need to go again as I've only just been so I ignored the sensation. I watch as several people are called into their appointments. I squirmed around on the seat and decided I would have to go if only to satisfy myself when I get there that I don't need to go. I was about to approach the door to the toilets when I was called back to the reception desk to confirm some details. Then I saw a woman with a small child go into the ladies.

Boxes ticked with reception and the

urgency to urinate has increased, the lady was still in the lavatory but I navigated the triangular sign placed directly in front of the door informing occupants that cleaning was taking place and that the cleaner was a male. I went in and stood by the sinks. Taking children to the toilet it is never a quick affair and these two were taking an age. I was hopping from one foot to the other, my knees were pinned together and then I began doing the ancient tribal wee dance desperately hoping they wouldn't be much longer. I then felt I wanted to cough, and in this current condition it would not be a good idea as I wouldn't just leak but the whole county would need to be on flood alert. I offered up prayers and they were answered when the stall door opened and the lady and child appeared. I did not have time for niceties and I barged through uttering apologies hoping that the lady would understand my situation. In my desperation I pulled down my clothes and my nail scratched the whole side of my leg, but what a wonderful liberation, the relief I felt by such a normal bodily function. It was at this point that the stall door swung open as I never had time to secure it and whilst I remained seated, the male cleaner mopped the floor in front of my feet saying, "Don't mind me".

In the Doctors room up on the examination bed, I assumed the position, tried to remain at ease as tensing of the muscles, I am told makes it worse and I prepared myself for the speculum which always reminds me of double sided shoehorn. Doctor Adams loomed in closer and then a, "Umm" is uttered followed by Doctor Adams getting a kidney dish and a pair of tweezers.

"This is new" I thought to myself. Doctor Adams leaned in and with the tweezers plucked something from my female territory which made me flinch.

"Sorry" muttered the doctor and then she

did it again, then put something into the dish together with the tweezers which made a clang as they hit the metal of the base. The rest of the appointment followed as routine but my mind was turning somersaults wondering what the tweezer thing was all about. Clothes back on and Doctor Adams confirmed that the swab would be sent off and didn't mention anything further.

"Doctor" I said, I was now thinking that it's something bad but she wants confirmation before saying anything "What did you remove from me with tweezers to start with?"

"You don't have to worry Rose, nothing to concern yourself about" she said kindly,

"I have to know, you have never done that before" I replied intrigued,

"Do you really want to know?" said Doctor with a whimsical look on her face. I nodded and she brought over the metal kidney dish and laying in the bottom together with the tweezers were two very sticky jelly babies which had got transferred from my bag, caught up in my spare knickers and adhered themselves to my intimate region.

Chapter Eleven

All this reminiscing is lovely but it doesn't seem to be progressing me any further. The paramedics are working on my physical body and apart from feeling like Frankenstein's monster being electrocuted with 1,000 volts rampaging through my body courtesy of the defibrillator, nothing further is happening. With horror I see the light has now receded even further and is withdrawing from me, it is getting smaller. Panic sets in, what now? I continue watching with a sinking feeling in the pit of my stomach. Don't go without me.

Oh, realisation has dawned, I don't get any more intelligent for being dead. The light, which I had mistaken for the angelic pathway to paradise, was a cars' headlights on full beam shining through the café window which had amplified everything. Mega disappointment. What now, do I ask at Customer Services? Is anybody else dead here I can ask? Is there a telephone number I ring, "Angel Inquiries can I help you?" I hope I get a better response than the last call I had to make for information.

Is it just me or does the proposition of telephoning a company fill everyone with dread? Not everything can be done on line and even if it could be there is always some hurdle, some question, some inane trivial box which you cannot tick because you need some information from a living person which you cannot get hold of which then makes the whole thing void. Twenty minutes of your life (and believe me I'd like another twenty minutes and then I could say goodbye to Maisie) that you cannot get back, time completely wasted.

I required some information in order to complete a transaction at my bank. My computer had developed a glitch and I had physically gone to the bank in order to settle a problem. I approached the door of my bank to find only one harassed cashier on duty with a stream of customers in line winding their way around the bank like spaghetti, waiting patiently to be seen. In the time that I appraised the scene another two customers joined the queue so I hurriedly stepped into place. Movement was slow, painfully slow, I was temporarily encouraged when another cashier joined the desk, but depleted again when the first cashier took it as her cue to leave her position. Other bank members were continuously milling about but as far as I could see not actually doing anything. One poor girl was assigned to go down the line of customers asking if she could help but having to refer everything back to the counter, so why couldn't they put another person on the counter?

Hurray it was my turn, in the time I had stood there my hair had grown another inch, another frown line appeared and around the country another 100 babies had been born, but, yee-hah, it's my turn.

"I would like to transfer some money from this account to that one." I said indicating each account number,

"Did you know that you can do that online?" was the reply without her taking any notice of my paperwork.

"Yes, but my computer is unavailable at the moment" I said,

"You can do this outside at the ATM" she said pointing towards the door, she still hasn't even looked at me at the point,

"I wish to do this and then I have some

other business to sort." I said feeling as if I had to justify my presence. With what I can only describe as a, "Huff" she takes the paperwork, my mind did wonder whether she was any relation to Neanderthal Norman at this juncture.

"How much to be transferred?" she asked and then said, "Do you have a mobile phone? I can put the App on your phone so you can do it with a swipe of your finger?" then I got the practiced smile, which scared me.

"No thank you. I would rather come into the bank to do my business. I would also like to set up a payment from this account to pay for this and I have something which has appeared on my statement that I want clarified please."

"You could do all this online" said the cashier of the year,

"I could do, but as I have already said I have

no access to my computer at the moment." I saw the cashier open her mouth so carried on, "and I do not want the App on my phone and neither do I want to stand outside trying to distinguish the characters on the ATM screen which has been conveniently placed so the sunlight shines directly on it." I got nothing but a chilling look for that but any victory I may have felt was quickly quashed when she looked at the statement and said,

"You will have to telephone in for that."

"Why?"

"I am not authorised to do that on the counter"

"Can somebody else do it?" I asked as nicely as I could but I was getting a little exasperated and was starting to feel a little unwell.

"We have no staff available for that at the moment, would you like to make an appointment?"

"No I don't want to make an appointment because I am already here. Can't you just tell me what this entry is about please and then I may be able to fathom out enough to do it online once I get my computer sorted". I was about to beg when I saw a chink in her armour and she relented a little,

"What is your date of birth?" I told her although she must already know,

"What is your mother's maiden name?" I told her,

"What is the name of your first pet?" I told her,

"How much money do you have coming into this account each month?" I whispered to her, "Sorry I can't hear you can you repeat?" she said acidly, I repeated louder and I heard the man in the queue behind me say,

"You would think she would dress better when she has that much coming in". I want to reply that it's not what comes in that's the problem it's what goes out. My bank account is an abyss, a black hole, as soon as anything goes into it, it disappears for eternity.

My head had started to become a bit swimmy, I could feel a headache coming upon me, and I really just wanted to sit down somewhere quiet.

"How much goes out on your mortgage?" However many more questions was she going to ask? What colour were my knickers? Do I believe in aliens? I have been a member of this bank longer than the X factor has been on TV and I am still having to prove who I am. I told her how much my mortgage was to which she answered, "Was that £753.06?" That was enough for me, my eye was starting to hurt from the pain sliding over it and my body was being to ache. I said loudly,

"There is a person sitting over the road in the tea rooms who didn't hear that, would you like to repeat the answers to all the questions I'm sure some of the people here may have forgotten some of the replies!" There was a distinct gasp followed by a chuckle from the queue. I glared at her, gathered up my documents and left the counter. Walking out of the bank I saw a poster of a smiley fresh-faced young girl with a slogan that read, "Nothing is too much trouble. The Bank that's here to help".

I felt poorly and once I got outside into the harsh glaring sunshine my eyes started to water and nose started to run. I sniffed, very unladylike but I had no option, I felt in my bag for a tissue, my eyes were streaming and I couldn't see and I had an explosion of snot from three sneezes on the trot. I had so much slime over my face at this point I was surprised no one offered me slug pellets. My fingers touched soft paper and I grabbed at it and pulled it from my bag in time to catch another sneeze. I wiped my nose and my face and when I looked up several pairs of eyes were looking at me strangely. I looked at my tissue and found out I had wiped my face on my emergency sanitary towel.

It seemed to take an age to get home and I thankfully sank into a chair without even taking my jacket off. My whole body now ached, the only thing which didn't hurt were my eyelashes. If my visit to the bank had accomplished my task I may have felt better but I still had the anomaly on my statement to sort out and I didn't feel I could leave it in case someone was helping themselves to my money.

I psyched myself up, I prepared myself, tissues, book to read, pen, paper, documents, cup of tea and even a sandwich and crisps because I knew it would be a long haul. I dialled the number and I couldn't believe my luck, it was answered, but my joy was short lived, "You are currently 27th in the queue. You may wish to visit our website or pop into your local branch, otherwise please hold until one of our operatives becomes available".

I read most of Tolstoy's War and Peace whilst waiting for my call to be answered and uplifting music was continuously played, I now feel confident I could recite all the words to Nessun Dorma even though I don't speak Italian or know what it means. My waiting was been interspersed with a message stating how much they valued my call but giving me the option of calling back and going through all this stress again, or emailing them at, notbothered2ansacall@bored.con. I am politely told that they are experiencing large volumes of calls at the current time but I am important so to carry on holding.

The music then got extremely irritating and I wondered how important I have to be to actually speak to someone and then there is was a spark of expectation when I finally got a different message, a further impersonal, automated list of options delivered in a monotone voice.

Press one for another condescending message,

Press two if we can sell you something,

Press three if you are thinking of leaving us,

Press four if you are still awake.

I noticed there was no option for, "I want to speak to an actual person because I need help and my query does not fit into any of the above" so therefore I pressed two as I believed that if they think they are going to sell you a further product they will answer promptly and I was correct. A very effervescent "Hello you are speaking to Tristan may I just confirm a couple of security questions before we go further?" answered with well-rehearsed grace.

"Hello Tristan" I said with relief and before I could say anything more,

"Please confirm your name, address, account number, and security code number, the third and seventh letter of your password and your place of birth" this I duly substantiate. "What can I help you with today?" I explained my situation and that I just wanted an entry on my statement validated. After the lengthy wait I couldn't believe that I was soon to end my quest and I felt resplendent like Boudicca after a battle, the conclusion was on the horizon. I heard tapping and then a deep exhale of breath. "I am sorry but our computer appears to be down at the moment could you ring back at another time?"

The dent is still in the wall where I threw the phone.

Chapter Twelve

I notice Wendy coming into Costrights. Her sylph like figure darting over to the fresh fruit and vegetables. I bet she's going to make herself a healthy smoothie full of anti-oxidants and boosters for high energy workouts, no sneaky chocolate bars or jam donuts for her. Wendy ran the Pilates class I attended once a week and her class was secretly referred to as "Bendy Wendy's".

"People we have a new recruit. Please welcome Ambrose". She said last week. There was a shocked silence and then a mumble of,

"Hello." from somewhere in the room.

If I had thought of the name Ambrose I would have pictured a Father Christmas rotund type character with twinkling eyes and rosy cheeks but the vision which presented itself was totally different.

Ambrose was in his thirties, and had so much hardware piercing his face that if he had walked passed a magnet he would have been hard pressed to extricate himself. He had a stretcher thing in his earlobe which meant I could see the room behind him and I had to fight a compulsion to flick something through it like a hoopla game. He was also covered in tattoos. No part of the flesh which was on show was devoid of a motif, and no theme or particular subject dominated. His body was illustrated like a child's colouring book. My attention was drawn to a dragon's head which poked out of his armpit and curled around his shoulder. I was hypnotised by the image and was held spellbound just gawking at it. He noticed my idiotic gaze and said, "That's George".

"Oh my god he names his tattoos" I thought and then realised that I had spoken the words and not just thought them. He was just staring at me, I think he raised his eyebrows but only one of them was operational the other had a staple through it so was immovable. I didn't know where to look, this didn't look the sort of bloke I wanted to upset.

"Yes I do." he said,

"What?"

"Name my tattoos." My face blazed crimson,

"Look I'm sorry, it was rude of me. I'm not

usually so blunt." I am actually but he didn't have to know that.

Thankfully at that point Bendy Wendy started the class and I was able to drift away from him to my mat in the corner. Placed specifically so no one can look at my backside when I'm doing the exercises. Ambrose joined the front line, it meant I could read and look at all his body art without him knowing. He was physically very strong and it was obvious he was no stranger to Pilates, knowing all the positions and holding them as long as the instructor with no effort at all. I was quite envious he should be so good.

A sweaty hour later and my muscles which lay nicely unused for 6 days had had their weekly torture. I kid myself that it's doing some good but an hour's exercise once a week is hardly going to turn me into Jessica Ennis-Hill.

My face glistened with effort, and the long

T-shirt I had on which camouflaged my pot belly had stuck to me and I looked like I'd eaten a hippopotamus. I bumped into Ambrose going out through the door. "I'm sorry," I say, "again" and smile with what I hoped he would accept as genuine sincerity.

"No problem" he grinned,

"You are obviously not new to Pilates Ambrose" I say hoping to show an interest and not come across as a total old bag.

"Used to go yoga three times a week where I used to live. Moved here and saw the poster for Pilates and thought I'd give it a try." He opened a bottle of flavoured water and gulped down several mouthfuls, he had a tattoo of a man on his Adam's apple and as he drank the man looked like he was jumping up and down. I was trying to think of something further to say when he offered additional information, "I have just got a job here and it made sense to move closer. Heaven's Gate you know it?"

"Heaven's Gate! Yes I know it, visit quite frequently as a matter of fact" I said trying to hide my surprise,

"Love dealing with people, especially the older folk, real laugh some of them they are. Remember George?" at this point he pointed to the armpit dragon and I nodded embarrassed, "I looked after him for four years, lovely old bloke had a thing about dragons so when he passed I had this done to keep him with me. This one here" he pointed to lipstick on his forearm, "was for Elsie, never without her lippy, on the day she died she had a stroke and couldn't communicate but I knew she wanted her lippy on. I saw you look at this one," he pointed to his throat, "that was for Doug he was a window cleaner. Each image represents someone special to me. In the early days I used to tell them they could pick the area of the body for their memorial tattoo but some of the old gals were a bit fruity and all *that* space got used up, if you know what I mean." he winked and smiled.

Now I felt like a supreme bitch with honours. I was making assumptions about this chap and the more I spoke to him the more I warmed to him. His appearance was fierce but his heart was genuine and as we are always told, but fail to appreciate at times, it's what is on the inside that counts. Still, I couldn't get over that spike on his chin though, anyone going to kiss him would be impaled on it and he would never be able to blow up a balloon should he want to.

My one and only venture into the world of tattoos happened a couple of years back. I had been searching for an image to sum up my aspiration in life and I decided to have a Hawaiian sunset. A red, orange and yellow spectacle illuminating the sky with turquoise water ebbing and flowing up on the sandy beach, sea foam lapping and caressing the feet of a female in silhouette, whilst she gazes at the panorama, a tropical paradise and somewhere to escape to. I could see it in my mind but could never quite find the image to match up until I was putting my rubbish out on a windy day and a flyer smacked me in the face. I peeled it off and there, in all its glory, was the very design I was after.

The flyer was for a casino night in one of the hotels and the catchphrase was, "You are only one win away from paradise". This was it, the colours, the silhouette it was all there, perfect. I believed this was a sign and took myself off to, "Inkers and Art-text" the Tattooist tucked away opposite the chip shop and up the stairs and over, "Bob's Bits" the antique come junk shop.

A few weeks ago I had an unnerving encounter whilst walking towards Bob's Bits. I was ambling home, for once not hurrying like a whirlwind but taking my time and meandering along browsing in the shop windows and I caught sight of a strange looking woman in the doorway of Bob's Bits. She was dishevelled and un-coordinated, her coat buttons were straining to contain her and a purple scarf and yellow spotted leggings together with pasty type shoes is never a good look. Didn't this woman look at herself before she went out, what part of her thought this was an acceptable appearance?

As she seemed to be walking towards me I stopped and pretended to be interested in something in a display. I could see from the corner of my eye the woman had stopped also and it seemed to me she was observing me in the same fashion. All I kept thinking was, "I hope she doesn't speak to me" and I hobbled a bit further along hoping she would turn a different way. The Bag Lady, an expression which was a kind description of the individual and an insult to every bag lady there is, started to walk towards me again. It was then my one brain cell decided to work and to my utter dismay I recognised this apparition. Bob had positioned a mirror in the doorway of his shop and the Bag Lady was my reflection! It was one of those moments when you realise your own perception and vision of yourself is nothing like the way others see you, I think it was this startling revelation about myself which encouraged me to do something a bit wild and book the tattoo.

Not ever having been a visitor of a tattooist's establishment I was surprised to find an airy expanse with windows letting in lots of light and sections zoned off with equipment stations for both tattoos and piercings and partitions for privacy, a smart waiting area and a reception desk. It looked more like an elite spa. Big Edd, proprietor, approached the desk. "Can I help you?"

"I have this picture and as I have never had

a tattoo I would like to talk to someone and probably book in". I waived the flyer under his nose as I spoke. Big Edd looked over the picture, "I can't see this being a problem. Let me take you over to somewhere more private, where do you want this image?" He gestured to the sitting area and we sat and discussed the impending perforation.

"I want it along the bottom of my back just over my backside with the sandy beach and water fading out down my buttocks." I cringed as I said the words, I felt a little uneasy speaking to a complete stranger about my posterior but Big Edd was a true professional.

"I think that this can be accomplished free-hand as there are no hard lines in the design. Can I do the work or would you prefer a female to carry out the work? You can, of course, bring someone along to be with you" he said. I thought about it for a moment but decided that I was quite happy for Big Edd to do the work and as for bringing anyone along, I wanted to keep this just to myself until I was ready to show anyone.

"Obviously we will screen you off so you won't be on show" he said. I was feeling brave so I decided to go for it and booked the appointment. When Big Edd told me the cost of the tattoo I was nearly tempted to cancel the tattoo and fly off in person to Hawaii instead.

The day of the appointment arrived and I was nervous and excited. I told no one, it was my little secret. I relished the fact that, after having the tattoo, each time I sat down I would be sitting down in paradise although no one would know and it gave me a weird type of buzz.

With a confidence I certainly didn't feel, I breezed in the door and was met by a very agitated male who was rambling on in another language I didn't recognise. A young girl came walking forward, "Hello you must be Rose," she said and I felt better, "I'm afraid Big Edd is unwell today so Edouard will be doing your inking." The disappointment and fear must have shown on my face. Big Edd I felt I could trust, I made the assumption that Edouard was the scatty man who was roaming around talking nineteen to the dozen and waving his arms about, windmill fashion.

"I think I'll leave it" I said looking over at windmill man,

"Oh that's not Edouard" said the girl nodding her head to indicate the distressed man, "He's a customer" she hesitated, "he's a little unhappy with his finished tattoo, he didn't explain himself properly". At this point I didn't know if this was good or bad but Edouard then walked out and he was calm and reassuring and compared to the chaos the other man was causing, I'd felt myself relax.

"Beautiful Rose." said Edouard with an accent I believed to be French. He took my hand and kissed it, steady on, at this point I was thinking of the part of my anatomy he will be working on and panic began to rise in me yet again. "You have the image?"

"Yes" I fumbled around and found the flyer which was now showing distinct signs of age, "It's paradise that I want. This part on the bottom on my back, with these bits down here" I pointed to the picture and then to my body.

"Madame Rose I will get prepared, please go and lay down and remove your clothes. Then I will return and poke you" said Edouard, with a worried look I caught the girls eye,

"He means prepare you." she said, "His English is mostly very good but sometimes he gets it a little wrong in translation. His tattoos are wonderful, let me show you some of his work", she gathered some photographs of his creations, which were extraordinary and by the time Edouard returned I felt much calmer.

Finally I am on the couch, laying on my front with just skimpy knickers on and a Frenchman drawing on my nether regions. I hear the needle start and I brace myself for contact. Edouard had my picture set up on an easel to refer to but had already outlined the design. I was ready.

Just over an hour later and I was feeling a bit peppered by this time so I was relieved when Edouard put down his needle. "Madame Rose you have now been done by the art which is Edouard". Bit full of himself but I think I know what he meant and I was keen to see the result. The girl came in and brought with her a full length mirror on wheels,

"Are you ready?"

"Yes definitely". I said rubbing my hands

together.   I am standing there in my skimpiest pants, Edouard watching, clutching his hands together with pride as if he has just painted the Sistine chapel with an innate grin on his face, the girl moved the mirror round so I could see the reflection.

I gasped, my heart lurched, my mouth was parched, and I could feel the pulse in my neck. I couldn't speak, the words dried in my mouth. My eyes bulged out of the sockets, "What, what on earth have you done!" I screamed, "Look, look, LOOK!" I shrieked pointing at the tattoo,

"Whatever is the matter Madame?" coos Edouard with a frown "I have recreated exactly what is on the paper. Paradise as you have asked for".

At this point my normal countenance had gone and any attempt at being composed had dissipated into the ether. I was now a banshee in full throw,   "This is NOT paradise. This is paradise" I ripped the flyer from the easel and thrust it under his nose. "Look at this and now just look at my bum!".

"It is what you have", he said and shrugged his shoulders, and Edouard had a genuinely puzzled look on his face. He took the flyer from me and prodded his finger at the image, "Paradise". The girl looked at the flyer and then at my behind and started to giggle. I looked exactly at where Edouard's finger was pointing and groaned. I counted to ten and congratulated myself on my self-control as I wanted to use the piercing tool to nail Edouard to the wall.

The exotic scene I had imagined, and longed for had been replaced by two expertly and exquisitely executed large red dice with black spots on each of my buttocks each showing a six. Above was written the tag line "Throw a double six to score".

"Paradise" purred Edouard in a French

accent,

"Pair of Dice" said the girl laughing,

"Sacrifice" I had said as I advanced towards a frightened Edouard with the tattooist's gun in my hand and a look on my face to equal the Joker out of Batman.

Chapter Thirteen

The audience around my body were getting bored. No dramatic action was forthcoming. A little boy was pulling at his mother's sleeve, "I wanna play on the car Mummy" he was repeating over and over and trying to drag her to the kiddie's car ride which was to the side of the café and only about three feet from my prostrate carcass.

"No darling not today" Mother was saying, "The lady's a bit poorly and she doesn't want all that noise".

"Mummy the lady is standing right there" said junior and pointed straight at me. The boy could see me, this me, not the dead me on the floor! "You will let me go on the car won't you?" he said directly to me,

"Yes" I nod amazed, it was quite nice to actually be spoken to and not about.

"Darling don't be naughty. You can play on the car another day" said mother pulling junior away.

"The lady said it was all right" he was whimpering, "and the other lady was smiling at me", he dragged his feet as he was lead off. What other lady I wondered and then I turned and was hit between the eyes by a vision I had last seen 30 years prior. My Nana, my lovely Nana was standing in front of me, just as I remembered. Her home knitted cardigan buttoned up wrong, her door key on a ribbon around her neck, an apron tied around her waist and she was just looking at me with an amused smile. She was bathed in a shimmering blue light and then I realised it was because the freezer behind her was playing up and causing a spasmodic flickering.

"Nana", was all I could say but tears welled up in my eyes, you can obviously cry when dead. I wanted to step towards her but my feet wouldn't move. So she had been sent to get me, she never was on time, once left me thirty minutes outside the school gate because she had a cake in the oven.

"Rosebud", she said, she always called me that, she had been a fan of Orson Welles and I was named, at her insistence, after some sled in an Orson Welles film for goodness sake. "I've been watching over you. It's not your time yet, you have decades left and so many more things to accomplish".

"Nana, I want to come with you" I said and at that moment I really meant it. She looked so serene and I felt just like I used to as a little girl again in her presence. I wanted her to encase me her in arms like she used to.

"Rosebud, do as you are told", she said waving a mocking finger at me and it gave me an inner warmth. "I will come for you when it's your turn. Don't waste any more time doing things that don't make you happy. Bye sweetheart and I will see you again one day". Then she sort of melted away in front of me.

"Nana!" She had gone and I could feel the tears begin to fall, then the moment was spoilt with a sensation like I had been hit by a bus. My chest heaved as the jolt of volts arched my back. Someone forcibly opened my eye with a gloved finger and shone a fearsome light right into it. There were hands all over me all meddling and jabbing me. With the amount of rummaging going on I felt like the contents of a jumble sale.

To think this time last night I was getting ready to attend a leaving party for a colleague and today someone was very close to having to organise a farewell gathering for me.

Chapter Fourteen

Last night I had attended a celebration for a work colleague who was leaving, having found a better position paying a lot more money for doing a day less, why don't I ever find anything like that?.

Apart from visiting Joan and going to work I don't go out much so it makes a nice change to see a little night life. My wardrobe reflects the fact that I do not socialise much, being practical and hard wearing rather than pretty and party-wear.

I never have much luck when it comes to clothes even if I save up for an outfit it never looks the way I would like it to. There's always an extra bulge to accommodate or an excess of flesh to tuck away and it always looks wrong on me so I normally stick to bland and basic black trousers, the ones I wear every day for work and accessorize up with a different blouse for going out. You would think I would be safe with this option, however, in a hurry and late for work one morning I put on my work trousers, I had worn these out the previous night when I attended a combined wine tasting, limbo dancing and twerking contest at Heaven's Gate. My trousers felt a little tight and strange but didn't have time to waste and investigate at that point, then half way across the zebra crossing walking in to work, the previous days knickers fell out of my trouser leg onto the road. I don't think that pretending they weren't mine worked, and although the person meant well, shouting, "Hey Lady you've dropped your drawers" the incident still brings a colourful nuance to my face.

My figure which in my twenties had been hourglass but now was more pint glass and the one day diet of watercress and mung bean soup had not reduced my frame significantly but I decided against the traditional black trousers and plain blouse and for last night I did find myself a bargain in the local charity shop. A flouncy little number, which is a bit daring and unusual for me in a blue silky material with see through sleeves that had ties on the end and a low neckline, a little bit young for me perhaps, but as I would be wearing it surrounded by workmates I felt comfortable as I knew they wouldn't judge me or make assumptions.

To make myself feel special I decided to have a luxurious bath to start my going out preparations. I tipped in a liberal dose of bubble bath whilst the water was running and I watched with satisfaction as the bubbles frothed, foamed and reproduced. Looking at the ingredients and the description on the bottle I expected to soak my body in gallons of water permeated by the fragrance of freesias and gardenias which were infused with aromatic oils from the orient with top notes of lime. I was to have a sensual body experience with the seduction of my skin to leave it like feeling like porcelain and smelling like the Garden of Eden. I didn't know whether to bathe in it or marry it!

Washed hair, washed body, teeth cleaned. I would have painted my toe nails in an iridescent blue colour, the only colour I have which has not turned gloopy and thick but the last time I did that I fell asleep whilst waiting for it to dry and when I woke up I had a fat bluebottle adhered to my big toe nail and ever since then the colour has put me off.

Once body cleansing had taken place and make up was applied with the aid of a trowel to fill in the crevices, my rendered face looked as good as it was going to get. Hair done, although one side styled better than the other. I put on my floaty dress and sucked in my hippo belly and provided I kept in the dark I could pass quite nicely for someone celebrating their centenary.

I was wearing my glasses and trying to make up my mind whether to put my contact lenses in when my phone rang. As I am not of the generation that have their mobile phones surgically attached to their person, I looked around for the direction of the tune, which appeared to come from under pile of papers which were strewn on the table. In my haste to get to it, I stumbled over my slippers, put my hand out for the door, caught my lovely floaty see-thru sleeve on the door handle which jerked me back and my eyebrow collided with the corner of the door and imprinted a version of my glasses on the bridge of my nose and ripped the sleeve of my dress clean off. The phone then stopped ringing.

The missed call left a voicemail, a very helpful company wanting to know if I wanted their assistance to claim for an accident I never had. It did cross my mind that they probably caused several accidents by ringing at awkward times in the first place.

This left me in a bit of a quandary. Blue floaty dress now scuppered, my limited wardrobe had to provide me with an outfit to go with my black eye and imprint of glasses between my eyes. I hardly think that the latest catwalk trend would accommodate that look even I could afford it. Much muttering later I settled for a satin type T-shirt with a bit of bling around the neck in a similar tone to the purple and black colour of my swollen eye. Rather than the subtle smoky eyed look I was aiming at,

I created something akin to a gothic Picasso as I kept adding make up to my normal eye to balance out the look until it was so dark I looked like I was peering out of a letter box. The conclusion being I had to wipe off everything and start again with copious amounts of concealer so I then I looked like a geisha girl.

To complete the look, I decided against my well-worn black trousers and selected, from a vast choice of two, a pleated calf length skirt with an elasticated waist so should I over indulge it would stretch with me and Mary-Jane type shoes with a bit of a heel, which is unheard of for me.

I drove my very old car to The Rabid Fox, the venue for the shin-dig and I prayed to the patron saint of car parking spaces, St Jalopy, to find me a space close to the door as I didn't want to walk too far and, as my appearance was less than the perfect image I had hoped it would be, I didn't want to frighten anyone I encountered. St Jalopy heard my wish and provided me with a space, a very tight space up against a bollard. It meant I had to park close and climb over the passenger seat to get out but at least no one would open their car door into mine. It was a very warm night so I left the sunroof open a little bit so the car wouldn't resemble an active volcano when I got back into it.

I had a wonderful time even though the tights I had put on weren't quite big enough so although I pulled them right up so they were under my armpits during the course of a high-spirited version of The Macarena they started to slide down. Each time I jumped up and down I could feel the nylon edging further down my legs, by the time the dance was over the gusset was between my knees and I was walking like a penguin, thank goodness I had a long skirt on. The elasticated waist enabled me to put my hands down inside it, wriggle and pull up my tights, I caused quite a stir as people thought it was a new dance craze.

I had a lovely time and really enjoyed myself. The time passed so quickly and soon enough the festivities were over and the swell of people from the pub spilled out on the pavement and made their way homewards. Moany Tony from the warehouse had offered to walk me to my car, I was thankful it wasn't too far away as a constant diatribe of whining about everyone at the party would accompany the walk. I knew the end of the stroll would culminate in Moany Tony asking me out for a drink, because it did every time there was anything on at work. There must have been a nanosecond in the past when he was attractive to females as he had been married twice but I had a hard time visualising it. I kept trying to be polite about it but he cannot understand that I am not interested. He's perfectly fine to look at, has got most of his own hair even though none of it is on his head but growing out of his nose and ears and I am sure that in the correct light the gold tooth he has could cast a magical reflection, pity it is the only tooth he has.

I was fortunate to be rescued by the lovely Rachel who could see me trying to detach myself, she linked her arm through mine, "Rose is coming with us" she said to him, "and no, you are not invited". Brutal but honest.

Rachel, Sara and a couple more from work chaperoned me to my car leaving Moany Tony looking like a bloodhound dog, all deflated, his jowls sagging on the floor. I did feel a twang of guilt, but any sympathy on my part would reignite his ego and I would be back to square one.

Although a short distance to my car, by the time I got to it I had a blister on my heel from my Mary-Janes and my tights were virtually around my calf muscles. "Oh" said

Rachel looking at my car,

"Oh" I repeated, although it's not necessarily the word I would have used if I had been on my own. My car which was parked tightly up against the bollard on the driver's side was now also hemmed in by a Morris Minor on the passenger side. Absolutely no chance of getting into my car from either side. I hoped that the owner of the Morris Minor was in The Rabid Fox and was making their way back to the car but we hung about for a bit and no one returned. It was getting late and my heel was hurting and I was tired, then a flash of inspiration, which doesn't happen much in my brain. I remembered that the sunroof was slightly open, it is an old car and it was one of those sliding sunroofs and much to the astonishment of my colleagues I climbed up on the bonnet and managed to open the sunroof a bit further, after grunting enough to bring a wildebeest in from Africa hoping for a mate, I managed to open it enough to put my head and shoulders in. I thought I could slide in head first.

Why I thought this was a good plan I have no idea, but we can all be wise in hindsight. I slid in my head, shoulders and one arm, but then found I didn't have enough momentum to get further in and the aperture was not as large as the body trying to gain entry, so I shuffled and squirmed waving my legs about trying to edge myself further in. Rachel and Co, having drank large quantities of alcohol laughed and offered verbal help and issued degrading comments but no one gave me any physical help. The action of my legs waving about resulted in me catching the heel of my shoe in the hem of my pleated skirt and this together with the movement of an inverted human sliding head first through the sunroof pulled my skirt and my knickers to my knees at the same time as I flopped head first like a dollop of ice cream into the car, with my head stuck in between the front seats, my legs sticking out of the sunroof my skirt rucked up at my knees and my backside showing through the windscreen like the matinee performance at the cinema. All this showed my secret tattoo and my workmates got prime viewing. Sara shouted, "Anyone for a cheeky double" and all four of my cheeks blushed.

Chapter Fifteen

Whilst my body is lying on the very hard floor of Costrights and I am gazing about wondering what to do next, I see the face of a lady, which I recognise peering over at me. It took me a little while to place the likeness but I saw the squashed petit-pois on the soles of someone's shoes and by association it came back to me - the allotment.

Hallgreen, where Jeremy had been the gardener had laid aside their walled garden for use as allotments for the selected few. There were only a few cherished places and competition was fierce to gain a patch of soil. Jeremy, God rest him, was able to use his influence and secured an allotment for Alan, the son of one of the inmates at Heaven's Gate. Once initiated into the garden you were part of Hallgreen Earth Mentoring Projects which was the sign displayed over the gate at the entrance to the allotments (some unidentified person had taken the initial letters and scrawled the acronym underneath). To make the grade at Hallgreen you had to "Undertake to treat the soil organically and apply no pesticides, sprays or means which would comprise the integrity of the earth". If you were successful in securing a plot you had to share your knowledge of gardening and agree to teach or mentor other members of the project and share any surplus produce you had with other members and good causes.

On one occasion I had permission to go down to the allotment with Joan to pick some vegetables from Alan's patch for my own personal use. It was a glorious day and Joan sat in a deckchair, sunglasses on and directed me to vegetables she felt would benefit me. There were quite a few people dotted about including the owner of Hallgreen, Mrs. Margery Hampers who had once employed Jeremy and who was tending her own little patch and picking fruit to go into her trug basket. Jimmy, who I knew by sight was digging but not many were actually working most where leaning on gardening implements and chatting or sitting about enjoying drinks, the allotment had a sort of holiday feel, very tranquil and unhurried.

The walled garden at Hallgreen was divided into about twenty oblong plots. At each end of the garden a set of steps, one that lead down and out through an ornate gate to the main hall and was also the way in and the other set down to a part underground ice house which was secured by a padlocked wooden door. From time to time there was some activity at the ice house and Margery told us her friend's son kept certain heavy duty garden machinery in there which is why it was inaccessible and kept locked.

It was a warm day and although I had only been there a matter of minutes I was started to feel a bit sluggish and light headed. Joan although only drinking lemonade had got very giggly just like a teenager and even the other gardeners seemed to be acting a little strange. As I was looking at them it was as if they were in soft focus and I couldn't quite get my eyes right.

I sat down on the grass verge to have a drink and my attention was drawn to the ice house as there seemed to be dark vapour escaping from the crevices. I observed one of the gardeners closest to the ice house fooling about, which seemed hysterically funny for some reason. Even though it was a lovely day it did seem unnaturally warm. Then to my surprise one of the gardeners jumped up and positioned himself between the rows of vegetables with a garden rake in one hand and a hoe in the other and pretended to row, shouting, "I'm in a boat race, I'm in a boat race, I want to win!" Normally this behaviour would have warranted raised eyebrows but today it felt completely normal. Jimmy joined him and started pulling vegetation out of the rows saying,

"I'm going for a swim" and began removing his clothes. Joan was crying with laughter and then said,

"I think we should have a maypole, we can all dance round it." What is going on, and why had it got so hot? Then as if to answer the question there was a scream of sirens and a fire engine pulled up together with a cortege of police cars. Jimmy who was by now down to his underpants, picture ones showing images of chillies and "Too hot to handle" on the waistband was kicking earth everywhere believing that he was paddling in water, Joan was skipping around a scarecrow wearing a daisy chain like a bandana, I was in a hedonistic daze and I knew things were not right but I didn't care. Others were mostly catatonic laying in various poses with intrinsic grins on their face, but one or two, including Margery were clapping and singing, "Here we go round the gooseberry bush" as this was the closest bush that they had to a mulberry.

I looked over to the activity revolving around the fire engine and was then aware that the dark cloud emanating from the ice house was because it was on fire! Margery broke off from her warbling and was looking at the flames enveloping the outside of the ice house and saying, "It's so pretty, look at the colours", with a wide eyed expression akin to a Barbie Doll. A firefighter was trying to move her clear but she mistook the action for something more sinister and clouted him with a leek. Jimmy was filling buckets of earth, thinking it was water and throwing it at the blaze, in all fairness it was quelling some of the flames.

Several policeman filtered into the allotment to herd out the individuals. Margery was apprehended and handcuffs were put on the poor woman, not that she was bothered, she was thanking the officer for the lovely bracelets. The blaring siren prompted one man to run up to the police car and ask for an ice cream with a chocolate flake.

I don't know how long it was, or the events which lead up to it as I was stupefied and any logic thinking evaded me but I was aware of a trip in an ambulance, a visit to a police station and then waking up the next day in my bed with the most incredible thumping headache. Once I got myself half human I picked up the newspaper and was met by the headline,

"Marji's Marijuana Mayhem".

According to the news report, the ice house had been used to grow an illegal substance. The heat required to keep these plants growing had been provided by some old lamps, one of which had overheated and caused a fire which had burnt the foliage which had been on the verge of being harvested. The allotment and its inhabitants had been subjected to a haze of hallucinogenic fog which accounted for the peculiar behaviour.

On the plus side there was a quote from Margery who said, "It's the best I've felt in years, pity I can't remember it." A photograph showing a blazing ice house, a half-naked Jimmy, dazed members of the Hallgreen Earth Mentoring Project and Margery Hampers wearing her trug basket like a bonnet accompanied the story together with the caption: "H.E.M.P. Hampers Garden". I found out later that the newspaper had had several enquiries as to where you could buy these Hemp Hampers.

Chapter Sixteen

Prior to dying in Costrights I had been feeling a little unwell of late. I thought it was nothing serious and compared to expiring in the bargain section of the frozen foods, it wasn't serious, but at the time I did feel quite groggy.

I was definitely coming down with something. My throat felt like I was swallowing razor blades and nothing would alleviate the soreness which wasn't helped by the fact that every five minutes I would have coughing fit which would make the rasping even worse. I found a couple of stray cough sweets in my bag and put one into my mouth sucking upon it and hoping that I could ease the pain.

I had managed to make it through the day at work and was imagining a restful evening at home so I could feel sorry for myself. "Don't forget to drop off the charity donation Rose" said Laura. "she's expecting it tonight".

I felt really weary and tired. I'd forgotten I'd volunteered to drop off the promised monies. I'd offered to take it round on my way home before I knew who was taking delivery of it. I never did know what I did to upset her, but Marian never liked me.

Marian Wragg was the self-proclaimed president of the local branch for the Hooked and Needled Club. Where knitters, sewers, crafters and crocheting enthusiasts could get together and learn and share skills.

We'd had a monetary collection for a homeless charity in the office and Marian and her group had knitted and crocheted warm clothing to give out to people who lived on the streets. Anyone who does that can't be all bad I thought, so as I am an adult I concluded to just draw a line under any misunderstandings and make an effort to get on with her.

When Marian joined the club it was a little run down and the only participants were gossips who were more interested in learning salacious tittle tattle than acquiring further yarn skills. Even though I was not one of Marians favourite people I could appreciate the effort and work she'd put into turning around this band of like-minded people. As Marian was trying to drum up more participants and encourage people to learn these crafts she put an advertisement in the local paper, The Weekly Drivel. Either the predictive text on her phone had run amok or if the advert was made by telephone the signal must have been intermittent because some of the wording undoubtedly was incorrect and no one had bothered to proof read it.

The advertisement which should have read,

CALLING ALL STITCHERS

HOOKED AND NEEDLED

We are looking for new blood to join our friendly group.

No experience necessary as training and full instruction in all areas can be given.

We cater for traditional and unusual, the expert and the learner.

Come along and bring a friend for a fun time.

Then Marian's contact numbers and the place and time.

Instead, the notice that went into The Weekly Drivel read as;

CALLING ALL BITCHES

HOOKERS NEEDED

We are looking for new blood to join our friendly group.

No experience necessary as training and full instruction in all areas can be given.

We cater for traditional and unusual, the expert and the learner.

Come along and bring a friend for a fun time.

With just a couple of words changed the whole advert took on a completely different connotation.

The first week after the advertisement went

in there were several new members and one could actually knit, though sadly they tailed off when they found out the correct meaning of a hooking a treble, knitting two into one and casting off.

It was a slight detour to Marian's house and on the stretch of road I travelled there had been one or two minor accidents and members of the community had banded together to form a group to hopefully reduce or stop unreasonable and dangerous driving. A very good cause and one I am fully in favour of, however, on some occasions a little power can go to the head.

I was driving along observing the road signs when an over-zealous member of the society for the, Promotion of Road Awareness To Tackle Speeding jumped out in front of me with a speed gun in his hand, similar to the opening title sequence of a James Bond film, only rather than dressed in a tuxedo, he was dressed in jogging bottoms and a yellow tabard. I narrowly missed him and I had to swerve to avoid the idiot. I am sure that these procedures are supposed to be conducted from the side of the road not directly in front of the car which advancing towards you, his actions very nearly caused me to have an accident.

As I drove further onwards I encountered more supporters all congregated together in their matching tabards with clip boards. As I passed them I noticed they had an abbreviation for their group emblazoned across their upper backs which read P.R.A.T.T.S. I think possibly a little more thought could have been put into the acronym.

I arrived at Marian's house and stood on the doorstep. I was just about to ring the bell when Marian opened the door, obviously just about to go out. Her head was down and she was rummaging about in a cavernous handbag which was swinging open on her arm, she gave a little jump as she looked up and I saw me standing there. She had one of those faces that always looked miserable, the corners of her mouth were constantly down and when she wore her pink lipstick it feathered into the lines and crept down the corners of her mouth so she resembled a ventriloquist's dummy. Humour was a quality which had evaded Marian and she looked at me daggers for daring to stand on her doorstep.

My throat, by this time was absolutely killing me and I was moving the sweet from side to side in my mouth when I needed to cough and this wasn't a neat little clearing of the throat, this was a full blown hacking, the sweet slid to the back of my throat blocking my windpipe and then I was coughing, choking and turning a fetching shade of blue, spraying saliva everywhere and wheezing, whilst Marian looked on with a, "Get on with it" kind of expression. I thrust the donated bag of coins towards her when another urge to cough came upon me.

Struggling to get any air I coughed and via spittle propelled the cough sweet right into Marion's handbag. I watched as she disdainfully reached into her bag and in between her finger and thumb pulled out a very slippery lozenge which she carefully put into my hand and said tartly, "I believe this is yours". At the same time, Mr. Wragg (nicknamed Oily because his hair was so greasy) came home, took one look at me and said, "You're the woman who very nearly ran me over a minute ago"

Oh my god Oily Wragg was one of the PRATTS.

I can't imagine there ever being a time when I will make Marian's Christmas card list.

Chapter Seventeen

Looks as if I'm not going to see another December. Can't say I will be particularly sad about that part. December is all very lovely, with Christmas and expectation, a few days off from work, everywhere you look is full of exuberance and excess and then by the second week in January everything falls totally flat. Weeks of nothing to look forward to, just grim mornings, long, dark evenings, a large credit card bill and nothing but a void in the bank.

The elderly lady who lives next door to me has a house on a corner plot. In in that plot is a tree which every November is illuminated very prettily by fairy lights ready for Christmas. Her grandchildren put up the lights but by the time it comes round to taking them down in January they have completely lost interest and it's down to someone else. My neighbour Nelly, had heard the weather report which had stated there would be a storm and Nelly was concerned the lights may half blow down or start a fire or countless other reasons and having asked everyone else in the vicinity who had then had other more important things to do which couldn't be rearranged had decided I was her last hope and asked if I would take them down. I felt sorry for her, so against my better judgement I agreed.

Nelly sat in her living room which had a large picture window which looked out onto the ornamented tree. Although it was too cold for her to be outside, she would sit in her chair and watch me so that if I got into any difficulties she would be able to call someone. I did wonder why "The Someone" she would call, couldn't come and help me in the first place, but that was just me being nit-picky.

I'm not the youngest person to be doing this but I dressed myself in warm clothing, stout boots and as my coat was a bit loose I put belt around my waist to hold it against me. I had a step ladder but it was a mini one but I was able to climb up it and unravel most of the lights but there is always a part which gets snared up and no amount of tugging would free it. The bough nearest the ladder was sturdy so I decided to leap across the void with the agility of an elephant and climb onto the branch and then sitting down, edge myself sideways up to the snagged part of the lights. Nelly gave me the thumbs up as I manipulated myself onto the branch pulling a muscle in my shoulder in the process but was too proud to show that it hurt to Nelly. Gingerly and very slowly I moved towards the tangled lights and precariously balanced whilst trying up untwist meters of lead with very cold fingers. I glanced over to the window to see Nelly in her warm house sitting down in her armchair and I had to remind myself that envy is one of the deadly sins. Then with a buoyant flourish I managed to unravel the knot and was so excited I jolted forward and felt my backside leave the branch. In the split second I was air borne I envisaged the very hard ground beneath me and my very soft bones coming in contact with it. I squeezed my eyes shut for the inevitable bad landing and prayed.

I didn't fall! I wasn't in a squashed heap on the ground, and I wasn't sitting on the branch. There was no pain. I opened my eyes. Miraculously, I was suspended by my belt which had caught on a very thin twiggy branch. I was too far away from the trunk of the tree to get back to it and there was nothing in arms reach to grab onto. So there I hung like a Christmas tree bauble swaying in the draught. I looked over to Nelly and tried to attract her attention, shouting and waving, but to no avail, her head was tilted forward onto her chest, she was having her afternoon nap.

My audible cries did bring forward a couple of lads, one of which was the son of an employee at the recycling centre. There I am dangling in thin air and flapping my arms about like a demented budgie and one of these lads starts humming the theme tune from the Titanic film whilst the other, ironically named Jack, calls out, " You're flying Rose", and both of them snort with laughter. I can take a joke but in these circumstances, not very far.

Fearful of the earth beneath and that the twiggy branch had got tired with holding up a 13 stone fairy, my insides quaked when I heard the twig start to complain and creak and I felt it yield just a little, I screamed out to the boys to do something. Jack and pal then disappeared, Nelly was still asleep and it started to rain. Had everyone given up on me?

The branch splintered and I fell just a couple of inches. I wished I had on an incontinence pad as physical exercise such as this was not helping my efforts to remain leak free. I was relieved (interpret that how you will) when I saw Jack and pal reappear.

My little ladder was not tall enough to reach my feet which the boys had obviously observed but what they came back with was not what I expected.

Heaving it around the corner an 8ft inflatable snowman came into view. This had been part of an incredible Christmas display put on in the playground of the local Nursery School.   The snowman, in full regalia when completely inflated had been proudly wearing a top hat and carrying a cane but some of the air had escaped and now the hat was laying on top of his head like a flat cap and the cane looked more like a shepherds crook. "We couldn't find anything else and no one is about" said Jack, "We'll put in under you and you can fall on it."

The solution was not necessarily what I wished to hear but I was in no positon to argue. The boys engineered the inflatable in place underneath me just in time for when the twig finally decided enough was enough and released its hold on me. As I fell and made contact with the wet plastic, my legs went either side of the characters carrot nose and my weight caused even more air to expel from the inflatable at a rapid rate of knots and it sounded as if Frosty had had a vindaloo the night before. The expulsion of air did have the benefit of slowly lowering me to the ground for which

I was absurdly thankful. The abominable snowman had saved me.

Although Jack graciously helped me to my feet, the other lad had already shared several photographs via the social media he had on his mobile, face ache, witter, claptrap or whatever it's called, of me lying face down on top of a snowman, legs akimbo with a carrot nose embarrassingly protruding between them. It was at this point the fairy lights flicked back on and a pre-recorded message from a voice box inside Frosty reverberated into the air, "I've been watching you and I'll tell Santa what you've been doing." Nelly then made an appearance and said the immortal line, "That didn't take you long dear, I'll get you to do it again next year." No Nelly you certainly won't.

Chapter Eighteen

With a jolt which makes me levitate like a Victorian magician I am back in the land of the living. Racked with horrendous pain which pulsates through me I'm not sure that I wasn't better when I was in no man's land.

I am hauled onto a stretcher with wires and monitors attached to me, bleeping, buzzing and flickering telling the paramedics that I'm breathing. It all feels very unreal.

I am aware that someone is walking

alongside the stretcher. When my blurry vision settled for a moment I saw it was Oliver Sykes. The action of me looking at him started a barrage of verbal diarrhoea and he couldn't shut up. "I was amazed when I saw it was you. They asked if anyone was with you and when no one came forward, I told them you were a friend from way back. As you were on your own I didn't want you to be in the ambulance with no one, if you were going to pop your clogs at least I could hold your hand whilst you're doing it".

His evaluation of the situation was not filling me with confidence but I was in no position to speak as I had a mask over my mouth so I just looked at him. I did wonder why Marie had not come forward when the question of, "Did anyone know me?" was offered.

Oliver was possibly nervous so felt he had to fill any silence with a one sided conversation. I learnt more about this man in the trip to the ambulance than I had all those years ago on the college bus. "I'll just wave bye to my sister and her family", so she wasn't his wife then I mused.

"Remember when we went on the college bus together? I always fancied your friend at college, you know the really fit one with the long blond hair, used to sit next to you. Never spoke to her, admired from afar, there was something a little extra about her." Thanks for that Oliver, kick me even further why don't you, "but you were always so nice and friendly and I really liked you".

I couldn't speak but I answered him in my head. If I get the opportunity to actually talk to him I will have enormous pleasure to fill him in on the details. So he fancied my mate but he really liked me, so am I supposed to be grateful? That mate you lusted after Oliver, the one with the little extra, the blond you had the hots for all those years ago was a bloke, yes, he definitely did have something extra though I doubt whether it was what you expected.

"I wonder what happened to her?" he said wistfully, in my head I answered, he married a tea bag heiress. Just comfort yourself Oliver, every time you enjoy a cup of Slurper Teas you are topping up their fortune.

"I'll ring you from the hospital", Oliver called out presumably to his sister and then he turned his attention back to me. "Do you remember my sister Trudie?" I was able to manage a grunt in acknowledgement then one of the paramedics removed my mask and asked me some questions. Honestly I've already died and done a Lazarus and it's more important for the paramedics to know my middle name than keep the oxygen mask on me.

It was evident that removing the mask

wasn't a good idea and it went straight back on when I started turning grey so they turned their attention to Oliver.

"Do you know the patient well?"

"No not well. I know her name is Rose Mitchell, she's is 50 years old and she dyes her hair" Ok Oliver enough, they don't need that information.

"And your name is? Full name if you please to keep our records straight and it saves time at the hospital if you are coming with us".

"Oliphant Desiderius Dalrymple-Sykes" there was a stunned look from the paramedic and I could feel myself holding back a laugh, "I go by the name Oliver Sykes.

"I'm not surprised" said the paramedic.

"My sister got it worse she's called Ermintrude Nerissa Dalrymple-Sykes, she calls herself Trudie. I was jealous when she got married and became plain Trudie Smith."

"Didn't your mother like either of you?" said the paramedic with a bemused expression,

"It gets worse than that, just work out the initials" Oliver looked at me. My brain was a bit foggy, it's not every day, thankfully, I have a heart attack so I am allowed and then once I realised it made me laugh which resulted in me coughing and gasping,

"Your mother gave you the initials for O.D.DS and E.N.DS" I spluttered, "She really did have a sense of humour".

"My Mother's maiden name was Titania Farquharson she wasn't keen what it got shortened to, then she married a Dalrymple-Sykes I think it was her way of getting her own back" said Oliver with utter sincerity. After a short moment of reflection on Oliver's part and a brief moment of silence which was gratefully received by the gathered company, Oliver then continued speaking, "When we get to the hospital I won't leave your side. When you are settled I'll go and phone Trudie and then we will make a list of people that need contacting and things that need to be done. I can go over to your house and pick up anything you may need." said Oliver. Very efficient, and I'm sure he means well but I'm not sure I want someone I barely know to root through my stuff.

My mind is going back to my house and the state I left it in this morning. I didn't sleep well last night as I had things on my mind so in the middle of the night I decided to iron the clothes for today, my trusty black trousers had succumbed to over-washing and had shrunk and the waistband was cutting in, so it had to be the linen skirt which I knew had fallen off the hanger and was languishing in the bottom of my wardrobe, it needed to see an iron before it was worn again.

My compact and bijou house overlooks the recycling centre upstairs but downstairs I am not overlooked which is why I do not have curtains up at the French doors which look out onto my very small walled courtyard garden. The patio is four slabs laid outside the doors from my lounge and the rest of the garden only comprises a hanging basket and a thing in a pot which I was given, my whirligig washing line needs to be taken down in order to sit on the patio otherwise you would garrote yourself as soon as you stepped outside and someone with a weird sense of humour gave me a bright green frog which has a sensor that imparts a loud audible, "Ribbit" sound every time someone passes it.

Delivery men and the postman use the back gate and leave any mail behind the frog in a plastic box left specifically left there for that

that reason.

This morning, knowing that my neatly pressed clothes were on a hanger on the back of the chair I went downstairs to retrieve them in my frilly teal blue nightie and I was singing away and having one of those childish moments dancing away oblivious to anything else, my rendition of the Cha-Cha Slide is better than most peoples, when I heard the unmistakable "Ribbit" from the frog. Flustered, I fell to all fours and used the sofa to conceal me while crawled into the recess by the side of the French doors to hide myself from sight. I stood up and hoped that whoever had approached hadn't seen the floorshow I had just been giving in my lounge.

I heard footsteps going back towards the gate and I uttered sigh of relief. Then the postman's voice, "Teal blue looks good on you Rose". Horrified I looked up and realized that the mirror I had placed on the wall opposite the French doors was giving a full length vision of me hiding in the corner to anyone who came in the back gate.

One look at my house at the current time and prizes for housekeeper of the year have slipped well out of my grasp. For the first time in history I didn't have time to make my bed, I have the residue of a baked on lasagne fermenting in a dish in the sink. There is also a cake under an upturned plastic bowl as the tin I would have kept it in I used to rescue a bird that had been mauled by a cat, so I didn't feel I could use it for foody items again.

I am not a domestic goddess (Nigella and Delia are safe in their chosen careers) but I did attempt to make a cake for Joan's birthday. My very well thumbed copy of the 1970's Household Manual given to me by a very hopeful ex mother-in-law all those years ago had a recipe for a sponge cake which I followed to the letter, unfortunately after completing the cake, even though I was very pleased with how my achievement looked, I tasted a bit that broke off the edge and realised that some pages had got stuck together in my manual, (I think from when I attempted Jam making several years ago) and I had gone from adding the self-raising flour to three spoonful's of soda crystals, which I did think was odd at the time. I found out later that I had combined the making of a Victoria sandwich with the soaking of nappies.

The ambulance doors opened again and the other paramedic popped his head in, "Room for any more?" he enquired of his colleague,

"Suppose so. This one's looking ok at present what have you got?" he said nodding at me,

"Lady, nasty cut to her forehead, hit it on

the edge of the freezer from what I can make out, will probably need stitches",

"Bring her in" said my paramedic, I'm not sure this is totally correct but I am feeling ok so I don't begrudge someone else in need sharing the ride.

The doors opened again and Lady-with-gashed-forehead and another patient I was pleased to see came in. "You're going to have to leave Sir." said my paramedic to Oliver. I think Oliver was about to complain but saw the situation and thought better of it. He scrawled down a number on the nearest thing to hand which was a cardboard urine bottle and told me, "Hold onto this and ring me when you can." as he left.

Oliver Sykes what a surprise, to think I thought he was wonderful all those years ago. He must have a good heart as he was very attentive and he didn't have to volunteer to come to the hospital with me, but he does prattle on. I glance at the urine bottle I may just ring him when I feel a bit more like myself.

The other passenger was Marie. "Hello Rose" she said weakly, "It's so nice to see you err, um",

"Alive?" I replied, removing my mask for a moment

"They asked if anyone knew you and I put my hand in the air so vigorously I upset my balance fell into the trolleys, I've cut myself see!" she thrust a blood soaked arm under my nose.

Lady-with—gashed-forehead then decided to lecture me on dying somewhere more acceptable as I had caused a great deal of trouble and annoyance. I promised via nods and smiles to take on board her advice for the next time.

I was thankful when the ambulance door finally closed for the last time as it was close to standing room only in the back. Marie and Lady-with-gashed-forehead were twittering away to each other and getting on fabulously, I feel lucky that I am in the same world and able to join in.

As the ambulance drove away from Costrights I made another mental list. This time it was a life shopping list,
Mental note to self:

- Phone Maisie and make arrangements to go and see her.
- Organise a big celebration for all the people who mean something to me.
- Learn to laugh at myself, if I do, I won't be hurt by anyone else doing so.
- Treat everyone as if it's the last time I will see them, one day it will be true.
- Make time for my friends, even when it's difficult as that's when it's most important.

- Do not judge, or make assumptions based on someone's appearance, it's the inner person that matters.
- Don't wait around wondering, go for it, if I make a fool of myself so what, laugh, and have another go.
- Tackle all my problems head on, they may not be a bad as I first thought and even if they are, I will have made a start at resolving them.

Perhaps this was all a divine plan after all, to teach me to value the people I know and the experiences I've had and not crave unimportant possessions and superficial relationships.

I mentally speak to my Nana, "Nana I'm not ready to join you yet I have a whole lot of living still to do in whatever time I'm allocated".

I can't be sure as I am still at bit woozy but I believe that I had a shallow whisper in my ear which sounded a lot like my Nana which said, "Enjoy every minute of that world, it gets better and you won't believe what's in the next world!"

The End (Or a New Beginning!)

Authors Note

Obviously anyone can read this story but it was written with ladies over the age of 45 in mind as younger ones may not understand the references. It has been printed in a larger font on purpose so you don't have to hunt round for your reading glasses and the chapters are short intentionally, so you can pick it up and read a couple of pages while you are waiting for your dinner to cook as this may be the only time you get to yourself.

Nothing in this story is meant to offend or upset anyone and if it does I wholeheartedly apologise. Most of the chapters are based on something I have experienced, witnessed or had told to me first hand, with a little embellishment!

Males have a flurry of hormone activity when they go through puberty but women have a rough time with hormones all through their lives. Whether it's the monthly siege, trying for a baby, having a baby, trying not to have a baby and we have to keep going through it all usually keeping everyone else happy and working at the same time. Then "Us" females are hit by the sledge hammer which is the menopause and when occasionally it all gets too much and we want a tearful rant, we are looked at as if we are aliens by the other gender.

So, I address all you lovely ladies in the same boat, I hope you can identify and relate to some of the experiences. My other hope is that something, somewhere in this little story will raise a smile. If this story makes you smirk, chuckle, grin or even properly laugh, I feel I will have succeeded in making your day brighter if only for just a moment.

Thank you for reading!

References

Just in case the references on some of the pages puzzle you, you can look them up. (By the way it's only the 1997 film I saw when it was first premiered the others I saw 30 years after they were made!)

Citizen Kane 1941 film starring Orson Welles   (Rosebud reference)

Titanic film 1997 (Rose & Jack reference)

Whatever Happened to Baby Jane 1962 (Jane & Blanche Hudson reference)

Printed in Great Britain
by Amazon

50148275R00116